Fred Khumalo

Talk of the Town

KWELA BOOKS

KWELA Books,
an imprint of NB Publishers,
40 Heerengracht, Cape Town, South Africa
PO Box 879, Cape Town, South Africa, 8000
www.kwela.com

Cover design by publicide
Author photo by Alet Pretorius
Typography by Nazli Jacobs
Set in Granjon

Printed by **novus print**, a Novus Holdings company

First edition, first impression 2019

ISBN: 978-0-7957-0898-5

Contents

Talk of the Town

We claw back to the past, where we find sweet memories hiding in a corner. We grab them by their ears, drag them out of their hideout and ask them to speak to us. *Speak to us, memories, speak to us!*

The memories open their mouths and speak: Mpumalanga township, KwaZulu-Natal, circa 1979. You are ten years of age. The neighbours are still salivating over a brand-new kitchen scheme from Ellerines that was delivered to your house at the end of October the previous year. Your mother had bought it along with an equally enviable dining-room suite from Town Talk.

A splendiferous Christmas is inevitable. Neighbours and relatives from afar converge on the four-roomed house that your mother calls 'My Castle'. They 'oooh' and 'aaah' over the new acquisitions. Your mother swells with pride, like a vetkoek made of self-raising flour.

The heaps of praises embolden her to show them further acts of munificence. She bakes them the tastiest, succulent scones on her new Glenwood coal stove, which she bought, also from Town Talk, two years ago. She's already paid it off, she doesn't omit to remind them. More 'ooohs' and 'aaahs'.

But you know that some of the 'ooohs' and 'aaahs' are not

genuine. Some of the 'ooohs' and 'aaahs' come from hearts that are as harsh and bitter as the juice of the aloe. Not so long ago you overheard two women from the neighbourhood – here they are now, sitting on your mother's sofas, drinking your mother's tea, sweetening it with shovelfuls of your mother's sugar – talking to each other, oblivious of you and your friends playing nearby.

WOMAN NO. 1: 'Who does she think she is? Buying from two stores at the same time? She's just showing off.'

WOMAN NO. 2: 'How come the repossession trucks have never stopped at her door?'

WOMAN NO. 1: 'Maybe she's got umuthi to ward off bad luck.'

WOMAN NO. 2: 'But she can't be using umuthi. She's educated. I hear she's got JC.'

WOMAN NO. 1: 'What has that Junior Certificate done for her? Ten years of school, for what? She works in white people's kitchens, just like the rest of us. And the educated ones are the most dangerous when it comes to the use of umuthi. They will bewitch you yet.'

You are wondering what your mom's education and umuthi have got to do with the furniture she's just bought. But you say nothing, because the mind of a grown-up works in mysterious ways.

January comes. You and your siblings go back to school. Some children are not so lucky. No money to go back. In the paroxysms of excitement over the Christmas season, their parents bought lots of meat and drinks and music records and more meat and drinks and music records and more drinks, which they drank and drank and drank until they forgot to set aside money for school fees, and even their own bus fares for going back to work in the new year.

Anyway, in February you notice that your mother's tummy is big again. *Damn these siblings,* you curse, *why do they put themselves in my mummy's stomach knowing very well that at some stage they will come out! When they come out, what will the harvest be? Where do they think they are going to sleep?*

There are already five of you – seven, including your parents – in the two-bedroomed house that your mother calls 'My Castle'. In addition, there's a constant traffic of aunts, uncles, cousins, grandfathers, grandmothers, and all their cousins, uncles, aunts who come from the country somewhere, to spend weeks, sometimes months, here at your house while they look for work in town.

Anyway, May, June, July thereabouts, your mom has stopped going to work. She must attend to the bloody growing tummy. The men from Town Talk and Ellerines come on their scooters to collect money for the furniture. Since the end of February, you've seen trucks from these two stores descending on the neighbourhood, to repossess furniture that was bought last November.

That's how the hood rolls. People pay a hire-purchase deposit at one of the stores around November. The furniture gets delivered in December – just in time for the festive season. The proud owners of the new furniture invite the entire neighbourhood to come and enjoy the new sofas and kitchen scheme and gumba-gumba music system. All of which gets repossessed for non-payment in February or March. It used to be a scandal to have one's furniture repossessed. Not any more. It's the ones who do not have their furniture repossessed who now get looked at askance. The neighbourhood hisses at them: 'Nxx! Bazenza ngcono. They think they are better!'

But the trucks from the furniture stores don't bother you because your mom has always paid the scooter men with a smile. Sometimes she even goes to town herself and pays the money over the counter at Town Talk. You know this because you once accompanied her on one such visit to Town Talk. She pays the money in cash to a clerk who beams at her, nodding approvingly. Then the clerk gives your mom a huge packet of sweets and a handful of balloons for being a conscientious customer. A conscientious customer is a customer who does not sit at home and wait for the scooter man to come and collect the money from her at the end of the month. A conscientious customer is the one who wakes up in the morning, washes, gets dressed, walks to the bus stop, and takes a bus to town. All of this so she can pay, on time, her monthly furniture instalment. Sometimes your mother pays a month in advance. Where have you ever heard of such a feat! That makes her a Super Conscientious Customer, earning her a bigger supply of sweets and balloons. Of course your friends don't believe you when you tell them this. They are eating you jealousy, to use township lingo.

Anyway, when you get home and inflate the balloons, you notice they have painted on them the face of a puppet with a huge smile. The puppet is smiling at you and your mom for being Super Conscientious Customers. When you open the packet of sweets, you are in for a treat. The sweets come in different colours: white, pink, apricot and many colours whose names you do not know. They are in different shapes too. Triangles, rectangles, squares. Some are in the shape of a heart. A heart is a symbol of love. That is what they told you at Sunday school. You notice that the sweets have something written on them. Your mother notices you noticing the writing. She smiles. Her smile is sweet. Sweeter than the sweet you are looking at. Your mom tells you the sweets are called Zulu Mottos. You are proud the sweets are named after your people, the Zulu people. How sweet. Then your mother starts reading one of the messages on the heart-shaped sweet: 'Ake Ngithi Qabu!' *May I Steal a Kiss!* Lovely! A sweet that can talk. Now that you know the sweet wants to kiss you, you lick it lovingly with your tongue. You look at it. It is smiling back at you, in its heart-shaped way. Then you put it in your mouth. And start chewing it. It is crumbly. Crumbly in its heart-shaped, smiley way. How lovely to be a Town Talk customer. Not just a customer. A Super Conscientious Town Talk Customer. You get sweets that talk to you. That are named after your people, the Zulus. How sweet.

Sometimes your father disappears from home for days, sometimes weeks. Nothing really unusual. Fathers tend to disappear every now and then from their homes. They go to that horrible place called prison. It's a place where they keep criminals. Thieves, killers and law breakers in general. Except your father has never killed anyone, nor stolen anything from anyone. But he is constantly in trouble with the law because they always find something wrong with his papers. In this, he is not alone. Many fathers from the neighbourhood, who disappear every now and then, have problems with their papers. Their papers are never in the state the authorities want them. There's always something wrong with the papers. So they take you to prison.

In prison you hang out with the really bad guys. The murderers and thieves and assaulters and the people who talk back to the white man. And if you've been to prison, your name gets blackened sometimes. There is a man who has a really blackened name. He is in a prison that floats on water. You are not allowed to say his name. But your father, after looking over his shoulder, sometimes whispers that man's name. Mandela. That Mandela man talked back to the white man. He did not just talk back to the white man, but he pointed a finger into the white man's face and said some nasty things about the white man. Like how the white man is doing ungodly things to people who are not white. Doing ungodly things to other people is bad because it makes God angry, and when He is angry, He is most likely to send a person to hell. Hell, as any fool knows, is a nasty place. You burn and burn forever. And the fire down there is horrible. When you, ten years old, get bored, you sometimes drizzle some hot candle wax on your exposed skin. You yelp out in pain. Because it's sore. Now imagine being immersed in flames a million times the heat from hot candle wax. You get the picture. Hell is nasty. This white man must be very dumb to do things that might anger God who will then send him to hell.

At any rate, it is against the law to remind the white man that what he is doing to others is ungodly. The man called Mandela knows this best. He is now in prison. With a very blackened name. But everybody knows that when your father disappears and goes into that place called prison, it is not because he is a bad man. His papers just refuse to obey him. He tries to get them to stand to attention like good soldiers, but they have a mind of their own. They just won't stand to attention like good soldiers. He says 'Soldier, attention' like they do in the war movies, but the papers stand every which way and they start chewing gum and blowing bubbles like bad boys and desperadoes who have no care in the world. These papers simply won't play the game. It's not only your father who has trouble with the papers. Even the local preacher gets picked up for his wrong papers. So you see, if these papers can defy even the holy man of God, who is your father? You see!

It is during many of your father's disappearances from home that the nasty nameless brown stuff hits the asbestos roof. The scooter man comes. He asks: 'Where's your mother?' You look in her bedroom, because that's where you last saw her, reading a magazine and drinking tea. But now you can't find her. You wonder what happened to her. You've been sitting by the Glenwood coal stove in the kitchen, a vantage point from which you can monitor traffic that goes through both the front and back doors. After all, your mother's castle is not that big.

You tell the man you can't find her. He shakes his head at your moronic self and leaves. You shrug, knowing how you're always being scolded for being absent-minded.

You return to your favourite position next to the stove, where you settle for a slice of peanut-buttered bread and a cup of umbhubhudlo, sugared water. There is something to be said for peanut-buttered bread and umbhubhudlo enjoyed in solitude, away from the whines of your siblings. Where are they, by the way, these siblings of yours? Better finish eating and go look for them. Otherwise you'll be in trouble with your mother if they hurt themselves. It's your responsibility to look after them; you're the eldest, after all. But for now, focus on your peanut-buttered bread and the delectable beverage. Make the most of it.

When you hear a whisper, you shoot to your feet in alarm. You think the heavens are checking on how you're enjoying your scrumptious lunch. But it's not the Man beyond the Pearly Gates whispering to you. It's your mom, her head poking out of her bedroom, asking: 'Is the man gone?' *She's a magician*, you think. *Now she's here; now she's gone!* She must team up with Mshumbu, the local magician, whose tricks never cease to puzzle and fascinate you. Like the other day when he performed a trick at your school. In front of the children gathered inside the school hall, he produced an egg from his backside, not unlike a chicken. Because you were sitting right up front, he beckoned you to come over. Reluctantly, you got to your feet. A part of you was happy that the magician had noticed you, but another part of you was wary. You didn't want the magician to experiment with you, as the teacher says. To turn you into a monkey or something. But you got up, walked to the magician. He said to touch the egg. It was still warm. Not unlike an egg that has just been produced by one of your father's chickens. Mshumbu encouraged you to eat the egg – it was a boiled egg, he said. Again, you hesitated. You looked at the other kids. They were looking at you enviously, swallowing their saliva endlessly. So you cracked the egg open. You tore it into two pieces. Just to check if it had the yellow stuff inside. The yoke, as the teacher calls it. And yes, the egg had the yoke. Of course, you know it is spelt Y-O-L-K. But you pronounce it 'yoke'. The 'l' is silent. You wonder why they put it in when they were going to make it silent. Grown-up people are strange. So you had two pieces of the egg in your hand. You could smell it. It smelt like a proper boiled egg. So you ate it. It tasted like a regular boiled egg! If only you could get some salt.

Yes, your mom the magician must team up with Mshumbu. Together they can lay more boiled eggs. This time there'll be salt. There's always enough salt at your house. Even the neighbours come over every now and then to say, 'Makhi, I forgot to buy salt. Can I borrow just a handful?' You know they are lying. They didn't forget to buy their own salt. They never buy their own salt because they know your mother is a salt mine, so generous is she. Of course, you never say these things. Your mother doesn't like meanness. But, hey, some lines need to be drawn. Your mother is never someone to draw the lines. Anyway, she always has extra salt. So, when she starts working with Mshumbu to produce eggs, salt won't be an issue at all. Come to think of it, maybe one day your mother and Mshumbu won't stop at just producing boiled eggs. They will graduate to producing golden eggs too. Now, that would be Superman cool. Yeah, your mom the magician.

Anyway, two weeks later, the gate creaks open. Someone is coming through. Half-naked, your mom rushes to the kitchen. She says to you and your siblings: 'Tell the scooter man I am not here. You hear?'

You nod in unison.

'What did I say?'

'To tell the scooter man Mom is not here,' you respond with confidence.

Your mom smiles, then disappears into her bedroom. The man knocks. You tell him to come in. He looks hungrily at the dining-room suite. He plonks his huge frame on one of the sofas, and bounces on it as if testing it for firmness. He looks at the pictures on the wall. There's your mom and father resplendent in their wedding day finery. Next to that is a picture of a white woman. Your mom told you some time ago that the white woman is called Queen Elizabeth. You once asked your mom why the woman called Queen Elizabeth was on your wall if she was not your relative. But you were still young and silly when you asked that question. Now you know why Queen Elizabeth is there on the wall, smiling mysteriously at you. Your mom used to work for a white woman who loved Queen Elizabeth. Because your mom loved this white woman who loved Queen Elizabeth, there was no reason your mom couldn't love Queen Elizabeth too. Logical. Next to Queen Elizabeth is the picture of Jesus Christ. Now Jesus is looking at you. Not just looking, but staring. And it soon occurs to you that He is not staring at you, but staring at the scooter man. The scooter man looks away quickly. Why was he looking at your Jesus Christ in the first place? He must get his own Jesus Christ. These things are paid for. Your family is paying him for the furniture. He has no reason to steal your family's Jesus Christ with his eyes. Back off, scooter man, get your own Jesus Christ.

The scooter man startles you out of your Jesus Christ daydream when he asks: 'Children, where's your mother?'

Being the eldest child, you are supposed to answer. But your seven-year-old sister beats you to it: 'She's in the bedroom, but she said we must tell you she's not here.'

Water No Get Enemy

Ekhaya and All That Jazz restaurant recommends itself to clients (both existing and potential) through one thing and one thing only: consistency. Take their steaks, for example. They are always huge and rubbery and, unfailingly, excessively salty. Customer service here is a persistent rumour. You have to shout, threaten the beginning of jihad, intifada, chimurenga, toyi-toyi – all rolled in one – before Gift, the alleged waiter, lifts his head from the Lotto tickets that he is forever filling out. Then he will shoot you a malevolent look that says: *Why are you driving a wedge between me and my Lotto millions?* On the wine list there are some mouthwatering goody-goodies, but when you order any of the listed items, they are 'unavailable from supplier'. Now that's consistency.

Yet the place attracts some of the city's top actors and lawyers; some would-be musicians and writers; journalists and conmen (if there's any difference between the two). What's the attraction, then? The answer: location, location, location. You see, Ekhaya is the only remaining South African-owned business in the legendary Rockey Street strip in Yeoville. As a result, when you sit on the veranda at Ekhaya you are blessed with a kaleidoscope of human movement and a babel of languages. Next door is Kin Malebo Congolese Restaurant, where you can see the Congolese in colourful clothes, doing their kwassa kwassa. Cast your eyes across the road, and you will be rewarded with the sight and noise of Nigerian brothers arguing at the top of their voices from the entrance to the rotisserie. Next to this hangout, Zimbabweans are quaffing quart after quart of beer at The Londoner, or Time Square Cafe next to it. On the pavements, chaps from Mozambique are roasting chicken gizzards and peddling boiled eggs. Their women are selling mealies, chocolate eclairs and cigarettes; an Ethiopian guy is doing roaring business from his telephone booth where people pay to make and receive calls. All these things combined are a boon to the armchair traveller who, without having left South Africa, can have a peek into the lives of 'others'.

The parade of humanity on the road never fails to trigger a comment among us as we sit on the veranda. Or a memory, which will in turn give birth to a story. Ekhaya is about stories. Hence the place's appeal to artistic types, who come here for inspiration – a euphemism for stealing other people's ideas.

Now, there are storytellers, and there are Storytellers. One who fits in the latter category is Guz-Magesh, a regular at Ekhaya.

He is here again tonight. I watch him as he settles down on his chair and takes a sip from his whisky. He pushes his chair as far back as possible, the better to give room to his generous abdominal protuberance. A mostly silent observer, I'm ready to make mental notes for later use in a short story.

'You know,' says Guz-Magesh, 'I've just been to the toilet. That it does not smell very well is an established fact. What has always worried me, but something I have never vocalised, is that the urinal has a perpetual stream of water coming out of it. The faucet at the hand basin does not close properly. And the toilet is forever leaking.' Guz-Magesh sits back, scratching his clean-shaven head, clearly thinking of a new entry into the story he is evidently dying to tell.

Some of the customers start shouting abuse at Gift, the alleged waiter.

Guz-Magesh presses on: 'You know, just like all of you darkies around this table, I used to be careless and presumptuous about water – until one day at our Liberation camp in Angola. There, my awareness of the importance of water was occasioned by an encounter with a baboon.' He surveys his audience, realises they are leaning forward now. He smiles, checks his watch, and says, 'What time does the game start on TV?'

'Three thirty,' somebody says. 'But what about the baboon and water?'

'Oh, I thought you were not listening.'

'Do tell us about the baboon,' says the one we call the Snatcher. He is a hyper-active, diminutive chap with a deep Wesley Snipes complexion, and eyes that are always darting about, looking for action, looking for stories.

'You people do not understand the importance of water,' Guz-Magesh continues. 'We've had the land wars, the gold wars, the diamond wars, the oil wars and all that. What do you think the next war is going to be about? I know you're going to say: food. Yes, it will be about food, but there can't be food without water. The next war will be about water. It has already started. Look at those water boys in Nigeria. They can wash your car right there in the street, at the height of a water-rationing period. Where do you think they get their water from?'

He pauses.

'These boys steal the water, that's what.'

'Ag,' says the Snatcher, 'water is boring. Tell us about the baboon. Eintlik, eintlik, what story are you telling, kanti wena?'

Guz-Magesh turns to him. 'Listening is a skill you can acquire for free, comrade. You don't have to be educated to be able to listen. Nor do you have to be as rich as Motsepe in order to be able to acquire the ability to listen. So, sit back, comrade, and listen.'

Guz-Magesh was still relatively new at the military camp in Angola when they put him on guard duty. All rookies had to start there. When you were on guard duty, they gave you an AK-47 and a ration of ammunition. And you had to patrol the perimeters of the camp, on the lookout for suspicious movement. Liberation Army camps were forever falling under bombardment from members of the apartheid government's Defence Force. In hunting down members of the Liberation Army, the apartheid forces worked in collaboration with Jonas Savimbi's UNITA. The apartheid Defence Force, in turn, helped UNITA insurgents in their drawn-out war against the armed forces of the Angolan communist government.

Guard duty was not popular among members of the Liberation Army, as it could bring them in close proximity to the enemy. But someone had to do it. The patrols were carried out day and night. Those on duty always worked in teams of two.

When the team got off duty, the camp commander would count their bullets. If there was a bullet missing, the soldier had to explain why. If, however, there was a bullet missing, and the member brought an antelope back with him, not much needed to be said. In fact, the soldier in question became the man of the moment, a hero, among his comrades at base camp, for meat was scarce. But even then, the top brass did not officially share in the enthusiasm for the use of ammunition to kill antelope. 'We're not on a hunting expedition here,' they would say. 'We're engaged in combat against the enemy. The bullets are reserved for the enemy.'

The firing of arms was also discouraged because it might alert the enemy of their whereabouts. Because those UNITA bastards were good trackers who knew the bush intimately, they could hear the sound of gunfire from miles off, and then track the source of that gunfire quickly. And before you knew it, the guards would have been cornered and overpowered, their weapons stolen from them. Sometimes they would be killed or, worse, abducted.

'You shoot your gun only under extreme circumstances. When your life is under threat. When you encounter a lion or some other extremely dangerous animal' – that was the mantra from the top brass.

Guz-Magesh takes a sip from his drink, and continues, 'So, on this particular day I was with a comrade from the Eastern Cape. We called him Cofimvaba, on account of the village of his origin. That's another thing they did, the commanders. They always paired a township clever like me with a moegoe from some rural backwater. They would never pair two city clevers, never. They said we city clevers always got up to shit. Said we treated the war as just another game being played in a township street. They said the moegoes from the sticks were responsible and disciplined.'

A deep, throaty laugh erupts from Guz-Magesh's lips. 'But what the commanders did not realise was that, rural as he was,

Cofimvaba was clever. Clever in the bookish kind of way, if you get my drift. His head was bursting with information. Now that I think about it, it might have been exactly for that reason that they put Cofimvaba on night duty. He used to say things that confused and embarrassed even the commanders who paraded themselves as know-it-all figures. Cofimvaba knew about Martin Luther, the King. He spoke about Malcolm X. He also knew MacGyver. Not the TV MacGyver, mind you. The MacGyver from Jamaica. The guy with the big ship who wanted to bring all the black people from America and Jamaica, bring them back to Africa where they came from. A crazy idea, if you ask me. Black people are having it nice in America and you want to ship them back to Africa where we are struggling to survive! Anyway, Cofimvaba used to get so inspired when he spoke of MacGyver he would start singing a song. Said the song was by someone called Burning Spear. Went something like "No one remembers Old MacGyver, no one remembers . . ."'

Some of the chaps are chuckling, until one of them bursts out and says, 'Guzzie, it's not MacGyver, it's Marcus Garvey!'

'You bloody agent, that's what I said. Marcus Garvey.' He bangs the table so hard, the interlocutor jerks his head to the side as if he had been punched. 'You must learn not to disturb me. Don't jump onto my moustache, do you hear!'

Guz-Magesh sighs, and speaks in a controlled voice again: 'Anyway, Cofimvaba knew many other interesting cats, apart from the MacGyver character. He mentioned another cat called Amir Cabral. Another one called Fanon something or the other. I remember it was Fanon 'cause someone decided to call him the Funny One, on account of the funny stories Cofimvaba and the other educated ones used to tell about this character.

'Anyway, many of us never paid attention to all that name dropping that was done by the likes of Cofimvaba. You see, we went into exile not to learn about some deluded MacGyver who wanted to take black Americans from their country back to Africa. We went into exile to learn how to handle guns and how to plant bombs. Yes, so we could liberate this country from the oppressor. The Cofimvabas of this world spent too much time talking about dialectical something something. The Cofimvabas felt very important because they knew all those things. Where were they when the boers were shooting us in Soweto in 1976? The boers did not care if someone knew MacGyver and Cabral. They just saw a kaffir child and they shot. So we had left the country in order to learn how to fight back. No manga-manga business; no Fanon this, Fanon that.'

Guz-Magesh waves a hand in the air as if to clear 'MacGyver', Cabral and Fanon away. 'Suffice to say that Cofimvaba could even tell you where and when these characters of his were born. As if it mattered. But what must have really pissed the commanders off was when Cofimvaba, during one political education class, started talking about a place called Diaspora. He said the Movement was an inspiration to the other people in this place called Diaspora. So, the commanders started looking for this place called Diaspora on the map. They looked and looked, couldn't find it. It did not help that Cofimvaba started laughing out loud.

'"You are making fun of us!" they said. "This Diaspora is not on the map. Don't you know we are the leadership?"

'"But, my leadership, Diaspora simply means the dispersion of people from their homeland," Cofimvaba tried to explain.

'But they did not appreciate that. They told him he would be on permanent guard duty until we get reunited with those friends of his in his Diaspora.

'And so, there I was with Cofimvaba during our shift. Deep into it, after telling me about this Fanon character – who it turns out is actually not even an African yet teaches Africans how to liberate themselves – and getting me confused by it all, Cofimvaba suddenly started taking off his pants. He squatted on the ground, intent on taking a dump right there in front of me! I shouted at him to go and shit over there in the bush. I told him I don't want to step on his shit.

'"What if there's a dangerous animal over there?" he asked me.

'"Go over there," I told him. "A man who knows about Fanon and the Diaspora can't be scared of anything. People in the Diaspora do not sound like people who scare easily."

'He wouldn't budge. So I playfully pointed my gun at him and said, "Okay, go over there; I'll cover you." I also told him that the comrades who would come on the next shift wouldn't appreciate stepping into his poo. Only then did he move.'

'But where is this story going?' the Misunderstood Genius, playfully pulling at his goatee, grumbles. He is one of those chaps who analyses everything. He will analyse each strand of hair on your head if you let him. He is already in his cups, hence the impatience.

We all glower at him. Guz-Magesh continues: 'Come to think of it, had I allowed Cofimvaba to shit right there, in front of me, I wouldn't be sitting here, telling this story. Cofi's shit changed my destiny. So, anyway, Comrade Cofimvaba reluctantly walked over to the clump of trees I'd just pointed out. I turned my back on him. With nothing else to do, I lit a cigarette. It was against regulations while on duty, as the smell could betray your position to the enemy. But we did it anyway. I had to smoke to take my mind away from Cofi. *Why did he wait until now before emptying his bowels?* I was thinking. *He should have relieved himself back at the camp, for crying out loud!*

'I was exhaling slowly, enjoying my cigarette, when suddenly I heard a ruckus coming from the clump of trees where Cofimvaba was taking a dump. Before I could say, *Viva the National Democratic Revolution*, I saw the comrade running towards me, his pants in his hands. He was screaming his lungs out: "Heeelp! Heeelp!"

'So I said: "What the fuck is wrong with you, Diaspora! Where's your weapon?"

'Indeed, the comrade was running naked, pants in his one hand, but no weapon.

'"The baboon! The baboon! The baboon!" he cried like a motherless child, the fucker.

'So I said, "What baboon?"

'He finally reached me, and clung to me like he had seen a ghost. The bugger hadn't even washed his hands, and he was touching me. I pushed him away angrily, but his fear was so intense, he clung to me body and soul.

'"Comrade, I am dead," he said. "The commander is going to murder me. Help me, comrade! The baboon stole my weapon. It stole my weapon!"

'I was thinking: *What is this fucker on about? Is he drunk or what?*

'And right then, a baboon came barrelling out of the bushes. Instinctively, I fired off a volley of bullets. The wily baboon ducked behind a tree. Now, Cofi's words began to make sense.

The hairy fucker had my comrade's AK-47. Which could only mean I was also in trouble. Back at camp, they would ask where I had been when he lost his weapon and what I had done to help him.

'I did not have enough time to dwell on that thought, for the bloody baboon was aiming at us!'

Guz-Magesh looks at the faces around the table, his eyes wide. 'Can you believe the pluck! I know you don't believe me. And if you don't believe me, how would a battle-hardened man in charge of ill-equipped soldiers in the middle of fucking Angola? But there it was. A bloody baboon messing around with the property of the Liberation Movement!

'I tried to take aim at it, but before I could . . . Listen to this: the bloody baboon fired a round. And it paused. It knew how to handle an AK. That's when we ran towards camp. *No, this can't be a real baboon*, I thought. *These people, the UNITA people, have got bad medicine.*'

Someone laughs and Guz-Magesh eyes him sharply. 'I also laughed, when, not so long before the business with the baboon, we'd heard that Savimbi could change himself into a hyena. Yes, you'd be sitting in the bush, dreaming. And you'd hear the howl of a hyena in the distance. Then the next thing you knew the hyena would be right underneath you, trying to reach for your balls. No ordinary hyena would be able to do that. It was Savimbi under muthi disguise! But, until I encountered that baboon, I hadn't really believed the stories about Savimbi, the Hyena. I used to listen, just like everyone else, and then laugh dismissively, just as you are laughing now. *A man who can turn himself into a hyena! Come on, give me a break*, I thought. *I am from the township, not some backward village where they believe all that nonsense*. Ha! My laugh dried up when I saw that baboon.

'Anyway, by the time we got to camp, the other comrades were outdoors, craning their necks, scouring the horizon. They had surely heard the unmistakable report of the AK-47. They were all armed, ready to repulse an enemy attack. They chorused in excitement: "Comrades, what's happening? What's happening! What was that shooting all about?"

'"A baboon! A baboon!" I shouted.

'"What?" Commander Zwai shouted. "Two trained fighters of the Liberation Movement are running away from a baboon! In the name of Moses Mabhida and Nelson Mandela, what is this world coming to?"

'"No, Comrade Commander, the baboon's got Comrade Cofimvaba's weapon!" I explained.

'By now, the comrades who had gathered around us were laughing and saying: "Disarmed by a baboon!"

'Commander Zwai ordered the comrades to shut up and go back to their posts. We were marched to Commander Zwai's office. This was where we were going to be interrogated. The interrogation lasted about five hours, during which time we were stripped naked. One of the commander's sidekicks squeezed our balls with a pair of pliers. Commander Zwai and his two sidekicks, who were always suspicious, thought we had sold Comrade Cofimvaba's weapon to some passing villager. They tried their damnedest to squeeze a confession out of us.

'Then they decided to make us perform water-fetching duties, a task that had broken many spies who had been planted among our ranks.'

Guz-Magesh sips his beer and looks at his audience. 'When

I say water-fetching duties it sounds simple. It's not like you get up, go to the kitchen, fill a glass with water. No. You were given a huge drum, a fifty-litre drum. You rolled it down the steep slope, because the reservoir was located down there in the valley. Going down there was easy. You just rolled the drum down the slope, and you ran after it. At the reservoir, you filled it up. Then began the tough part. You had to carry the fifty-litre drum up the slope. Under normal circumstances, these huge water drums would have been drawn by heavy military trucks. From the reservoir up to camp was a distance of about three to four kilometres. So, like cattle, we would struggle up the slope, with the commanders wielding sticks, whipping our backs. Wincing from the pain, you lost control of the drum. It rolled back down the slope. You ran after it, caught up with it. The pushing, shoving process started all over again. It took hours. The commanders were kicking you, beating you with sticks and whips. Sometimes even shooting rounds at your feet, which is a contradiction if you consider what I'd just said about the scarcity of ammunition.

'Anyway, the water drum, my brothers, it was heavy. As I was pushing, blinded by my own tears, I found myself thinking of the water games we used to play at home. In the summer, if it got too hot, and the children were restless, someone would attach a hose to the tap and let them play in the water the whole afternoon. Now, I was thinking of that wastefulness, thinking how those children would have laughed to see me pushing a water-filled drum up the slope. I was thinking of guys in the township, attaching a hose to a tap and washing their cars at a leisurely pace, listening to jazz music, pausing every now and then to take a sip from a beer. Or share a story with a passing friend. All the while, the hose is running. This is your tap, this is your hose, this is your car. Who can tell you? After washing your car, you have to water your lawn. This invention called a hosepipe comes in handy. If you are advanced, you attach a sprinkler to your hose, and you leave it running while you go and see your friends in another part of the township.

'I was thinking of my mother's white employers who had a water feature in the garden, a huge feature in the form of a dolphin spouting water. I pictured that dolphin laughing at me as I pushed the water drum up the slope. Water, brothers – something I'd taken for granted. The commander's whip cracked. I was crying, cursing. I was thinking of guys from our neighbourhood in the township, those lucky enough to have bakkies. They would load a bakkie with water-filled drums which they would then ferry to their friends and relatives who lived in one of the outlying villages, where the people were stupid enough not to have taps. Yes, that was the attitude among those of us in the townships: you don't have a tap, you don't have a flushable toilet, you must be stupid. Now, *I* was feeling stupid. For two weeks, I did the water duty.

'The commanders were still convinced that we hadn't told the whole truth, by the way. So, I got thrown into solitary confinement. Once a day, they brought me a cup of water to drink. Just one cup. I treasured every drop of it, this precious thing, this liquid gold I'd always taken for granted. Every time I took a sip, I hummed my jumbled version of Fela Kuti's song, "Water No Get Enemy". I hummed, "If you want go wash, a water you go use . . . If your child dey grow, a water he go use. If water kill your child, na water you go use. Nothing without water. Water, him no get enemy!"

'Comrade Cofimvaba, I later heard, got stripped naked. Then they buried him up to his neck in a hole that he had been ordered to dig. I later heard that he had been left there for two full days, without water or food. Every now and then, a bored commander would walk up to him, pee in his face, saying, "Have a drink of water, Comrade Sell-out," to the uproarious laughter of other comrades.

'A week after my release from solitary confinement, I was working in the garden when I heard screams. I looked up. There was Commander Zwai and his two sidekicks running for their lives, towards camp. I dropped my spade, picked up my weapon and followed them, ready to offer assistance.

'When they finally regained their breath, one of the sidekicks said, "Shit, mfondini, so this gun-toting baboon actually exists!"'

The Misunderstood Genius is hopping up and down the veranda, laughing and spilling his drink all over the place. The Snatcher is furiously thumbing away on his expensive smartphone. We know what he is doing: he is writing a Facebook post, telling Guz-Magesh's story as if it were his own. That's why we call him the Snatcher: he steals people's stories, dresses them up in new clothes, and parades them as his own creations. I might go have a look at his Facebook post when I start to write my short story.

But it doesn't bother Guz-Magesh. His well of tales is bottomless. Guz-Magesh takes a swig from his glass. He smiles. I can sense words gathering inside his mouth, dancing on the tip of his tongue, jostling with one another, trying to stand in proper formation, so they can come out of his mouth in the form of yet another tale. But instead, he simply winks at the Snatcher, and starts singing, "Water, him no get enemy! Nothing without water. Water, him no get enemy!"'

This Bus Is Not Full!

Vusi is on a bus home after doing some shopping in Watertown. Though the bus appears packed, with some people standing right next to the driver, there's still a lot of standing room at the back. In deference to people who want to get on board, glaring at him from the ground, the bus driver gets up and starts shouting to the passengers, 'Move back please!'

Then some public-spirited people join in, one guy's voice rising above the din: 'Motherfuckers blocking the way, this ain't yo mama's living room. Move the shit back!'

An elderly gentleman interjects, 'Please, be patient. People are moving!'

'Who asked you, fucking cracker? Mind yo fuckin' business.'

Vusi, although he is used to this kind of language, still gets embarrassed to hear it being used in public places. Yes, he sees scenes such as these in Tyler Perry movies. Or classic Spike Lee flicks. Or David Chappelle shows where the f-word is the punctuation; where the f-word is the oxygen that gives life to phrases and sentences being uttered. But it's not the kind of language that would be tolerated at Harvard, where he's a post-grad student. At Harvard, you step on someone's toes by mistake, and he goes, 'Oops, pardon me, my shoe was in your way. My profuse apologies, sir.'

Vusi is getting excited – this is the America they've been hiding from him! He must make more frequent use of bus transportation in his peregrinations around the city and its environs, he decides there and then. On past occasions he has relied on charitable fellow Harvardians for transport to the shopping mall in Watertown, which is out of the way from the subway train grid.

Now he is looking at the guy who's just called the elderly man a cracker. He wishes he could, as they do in the movies, say to the brother: *Come on, nigga, pull out your piece and show the cracker whatchu made of!* He's hoping for a scene he will cherish, a scene he will engrave in his memory so he can relate it to his friends back home. Come on, you Americans, Vusi can't go back to Africa without witnessing a single fight. What will he tell the people back home? He can already hear his younger brother booming with laughter: *Man, you're a loser! Two full years in America and you couldn't even get featured in one of their millions of reality shows – or create your own show, something like:* In the Abundance of Water, the Fool is Thirsty: The Miserable, Celibate Life of an African Geek in America. *Yes, a complete loser, that's what you are.*

In his ears, his best friend joins the fun at his expense: *The fool lives in Boston, yet not once does he get a chance to date Tracy Chapman. Loser!*

Another friend of his is saying soothingly in his ear, *Okay, if you're too tongue-tied to date Tracy or any other American, if you're too unimaginative to even appear on their TV, couldn't you at least, at the very least, capture on your cellphone a real-life, fully fledged street fight or, better still, a real shooting on an American street? Capture the thing, put it on YouTube and prove you were indeed in America! Come on, stop lying to us. You were not in America! Anyone can buy a Harvard T-shirt. Go to a Chinese shop in downtown Joburg, and they can organise you a Harvard T-shirt and hoodie, chop-chop. No magic in a Harvard T-shirt!*

Back on the bus. Vusi's lips are salivating. His heart is thudding. His eyes are wide open. As big as saucers. He's not going to miss a heartbeat of the action.

It's coming.

He's from Africa. The hunter's instinct runs in his veins. The hunter knows when it's time to stand still in the bush, and when to pounce. It's all about timing. Anticipation. And he can feel the timing is right. A black brother is about to pounce. He can feel it.

It's coming.

Those doubting Thomases back home are in for a surprise. The action he's about to capture on his phone is going to go viral, thus landing him a reality TV deal with one of the networks. *From Lecture Room to da Streetz: The Intellectual with Afritude*. That would be a great name for a reality show. *His* reality show.

He's clutching his phone now, ready to put it to good use once the action has started. How do they say in the movies? Camera rolling! Yes, the camera is ready to start rolling.

It's coming.

Like someone watching a fast game of tennis, his eyes are moving from speaker to speaker – not wanting to miss a word, not wanting to miss the slightest piece of action. They are speaking so fast, these Americans.

'Hey,' one man shouts, 'you-crazy-ass-cracker, whatchu lookin' at? Move to the fuckin' back of the bus 'fore I show you your mother.' The speaker has a face that reminds Vusi of a maggot. If maggots could grow this big. Come to think of it, he doesn't remember what a maggot's face looks like. If it has a face. Maybe it's one of those animals whose face can also be its backside? Like an earthworm, which has faces on both ends. Faces that also become its backside. At least that's what he thinks they said in biology class. He never concentrated much in biology. He knew from the onset that he wanted to be a money man when he finished school. He's at Harvard not on the strength of his knowledge of earthworms and maggots, if these creatures have faces or not. He is studying High Finance. No profit in memorising facts about maggots. Therefore, the long and short of it, he doesn't remember if a maggot has a face or not. But, still, this man's face shouts 'maggot' – that's how creepy it is. 'I'm not gonna say it again: move the fuck back! There's people wanna get on the bus! This bus is not full.'

Four people climb in. One of them is a woman carrying a baby in a pram – or a stroller, as they call this contraption in the US of A. The woman needs help to get her pram on board. But her friends ignore her. To get their attention, she says, 'Shiit! Can't a bitch get some help get a baby on board a bus?'

Somebody – not one of her friends – finally manages to come to her rescue. Once on board, the grateful lady says to the good Samaritan: 'What the fuck you lookin' at? You haven't seen a black bitch carrying a baby? Whatchu lookin' at?'

The good Samaritan is an Oriental man who seems to shrink into himself at the unexpected onslaught.

Finally on board, these happy citizens of America continue to talk as the bus pulls away – in voices that pose a threat to an average eardrum – about what they intend doing when they get home. It's Christmas Eve, after all. Some last-minute preparations still need to be attended to. For the Big Day, you see. Their narrative is peppered with short words that start with 'f' or 's', as if these are the only words that matter in the dictionary, or the entire lexicon of civilisation.

Some gentleman then opines that, perhaps, just perhaps, it would be preferable to eschew what he terms 'profane and impolite speech' in the presence of young children.

At which one of the pilgrims explodes: 'Now I can see why they lock black people up. I know exactly why. Black people be talkin' among themselves, know what I'm sayin', mindin' their own bidness, and some cracker be tellin' them, *teachin'* them how to talk. Cracker, I don't wanna be arrested. So don't pro-voke me! You been pro-voking me the whole year. The year's almost ova. Is Chrismas tomorrow. And baby Jesus gettin' born tomorrow. And I ain't need no pro-vocation on Chrismas Eve. Hear what I said? I said: Nuf pro-vocation! Get the fuck outa my bidness!'

The scene Vusi will take back home to Johannesburg, the scene he will post on YouTube, the scene that will land him a reality TV slot, the scene that will gain him street cred back home, is just around the corner now. He can feel it.

It's coming.

'I'm a crack a cracker's skull ri' now!' another man booms. 'So help me God, I'm a crack me a cracker's skull ri' now an' baby Jesus gonna wash mah sins tomaraw!'

A woman jumps right in: 'I know them crackers be phoning the po-lice right now, tellin' po-po we be disturbin' the peace and shit. No, we ain't done nothin' here. And I been recordin' this shit here on my fuckin' iPad. So, brother, please don't go

35

crackin' no cracker's skull 'cos I'm recording everything. Shoh, you can crack a cracker's skull if he try to crack yo skull, thas for shoh. But right now, as shoh as it is Chrismas Eve, no mother-fucker be tellin' lies about black folk. Sayin' niggas started the shit. I ain't puttin' my ass in jail for no shit 'round Chrismas no way!'

This pacifist dampens Vusi's spirit. No fight on the horizon. The man who'd just promised to crack a skull has gone all sulky. The bus shudders to a stop. The door opens. A grey-haired man in a tweed jacket climbs in.

'Driver,' one of the brothers shouts, 'get the fuckin' bus going! Whatchu waitin' for?'

'We got families to look forward to, nigga.'

'We ain't losers like you, drivin' a bus on Chrismas Eve. Shiit!'

Curses fly around like confetti at a wedding party.

It soon becomes clear that the gentleman who's just climbed in is perturbed by the exchange of insalubrious words (the gentleman is of such demeanour as to trigger the words *perturbed, insalubrious*, in Vusi's college mind). The gentleman is whipping his head this and that way, scowling at these citizens who are speaking – no, *shouting* – as if there were no tomorrow. Clearly a decisive man, a man of conscience and high morals, a man of good breeding, a man of authority, a man of no fear, the gentleman does the civilised thing. In a firm, direct voice, he addresses one of the speakers, enunciating each word distinctly: 'Sir, there are young children here. Please. Mind. Your. Language.'

To which one of the women cries triumphantly: 'Ah, this here cracker's got a Canadian accent! True, he got an accent. Speak up again, sir. What'd you say? I'm tellin' y'all, he got a Canadian accent . . .'

Someone responds: 'What a Canadian accent gotta do with gettin' on the bus?'

Now, the ice that had taken possession of the entire bus begins to thaw. The people start laughing. Shyly at first. Then in huge, bubbly gales. Soon, the laughter comes like avalanches hurtling down the tallest mountains. Wuuu-yoooo-wwweeee-hhhaaaa-ghhhhrrrr.

'But, hey,' says one of the speakers, 'the white people in Canada, do we also call them crackers? Or we have a diff'rent name for 'em?'

'I guess they be crackers too,' the woman with the baby says. 'They be cool Canadian crackers. On account of all the snow over there. And those Canadian crackers don't have no beef with niggers, far as I know anyway. So they be cool Canadian crackers!'

Yooooo-hahahahaha-weeee!

Vusi can't help but laugh out loud. Really loud. COOL. CANADIAN. CRACKERS! *These Negroes are cracking me*, Vusi says in his heart, trying to sound American to himself. *They're cracking me, these Negroes*. COOL. CANADIAN CRACKERS. Yoooo-hhhaaa-ghhrrrrrrr!

The woman with the baby frowns, throws her piercing eyes at Vusi. 'Nigga, you laugh funny.'

From where she's sitting – Vusi is standing in the aisle – she sizes him up, a tiny smile on her face. 'Yeah, nigga, you creepy. You laugh funny and you wearing funny glasses, and yo hair funny. Where you from, nigga?'

'South Africa.'

She's smiling broadly now. 'Aha, I knew it! You a Mandela nigga!'

Vusi notices that the lady is a scruffier version of Tyra Banks. She's got a complexion the colour of yellow cling peaches that are popular back home. A better hairdo, some change of clothes would do the trick – make her a Tyra Banks lookalike.

But his assessment of Not Tyra Banks gets disturbed, by Not Tyra Banks herself speaking: 'Hey, lissen up, y'all: today is full of wonders. There's a Canadian cracker ova there, and now a Mandela nigga ova here!'

Vusi smiles, internally thanking Saint Mandela for saving him from ridicule, or worse.

'Oh, African nigga,' a woman's voice croons from behind where Vusi is standing, 'I'll have myself an African nigga any-time, baby. Any time.'

Vusi turns to see a woman with very unique features. Her face, chin and neck are all fused together. But she has beautiful teeth and kissable lips. She's not done talking: 'All my friends call me African Queen, I guess on account of my generous lips and overly generous booty. Pity you cain't see my booty 'cos I'm sittin' down.'

The laughter that follows is so loud, Vusi is scared the lady might just get up – to prove to all and sundry that she indeed is bootylicious. Vusi is not in a hurry to see the booty, if the face-chin-neck fusion is anything to go by.

Someone is muttering, clearly in reference to Vusi, 'He don't look starving, for an African.'

Not Tyra Banks comes to Vusi's defence: 'He ain't from just anywhere-Africa. He from Mandela Africa. They got elevators there, they got McDonald's, and big highways too. Saw it on History Channel.'

Vusi is swelling with pride. What the Americans have taught

him since he got here is: *Don't be modest, you ain't famous.* He must say something now. He can't suppress the need to educate these Americans. Those Americans at Harvard pretend they know all about Africa, so he never bothers to tell them about his country. Half Tyra Banks is very observant, indeed. She can tell South Africans from the other Africans. Vusi must take her mobile number. So they can stay in touch. Hit two birds with one stone: get an American who will listen with star-struck admiration to his African tales of conquest and civilisation, and also get an American lady who will date him, a lady he can brag about once he gets home. Vusi has been highly inspired by Half Tyra Banks's intervention on his behalf. When he finishes his studies, he will take Almost Tyra Banks back home to Africa – and tell his brothers she, indeed, is the real Tyra Banks's sister. Yes, he must talk to this woman who can differentiate Mandela's country from the rest of the continent.

He clears his throat now, puffs out his chest, ready to tell the more ignorant fellow passengers that the land of Mandela is not about lions and giraffes and starving babies and cannibals and people living in trees and Ebola. Mandela's land produces the likes of him, intellectuals of his stature. Thinkers who can converse at the highest level with the citizens of the world, cosmopolitan connoisseurs who buy their food and clothes at Watertown, not Chinatown, intellectuals who carry themselves with pride as they walk under the shadow of John Harvard. He is proud to have been anointed by Mandela to go out into the world and—

'Hey,' one of the black brothers breaks into Vusi's thoughts, 'let me guess: you a Harvard nigga? Or is it MIT?'

Vusi doesn't care for the word 'nigga' – black Americans will never cease to amaze him; why have they decided to embrace what used to be a racial slur? – but the inclusion of 'Harvard' in the man's enquiry somehow cushions the blow of the N-word.

'Answer me, nigga. You Harvard or MIT?'

This is taking an interesting turn. A pleasant turn. He had taken these people to be ruffians, the detritus from the pavements of Roxbury and Dorchester, the ghettoes of Boston. But for them to recognise him as a Harvard man, for them to realise that he is a Master of the Universe in the making . . . That's something. It counts in their favour.

Before Vusi can confirm to the man who asked the question that he is indeed a proud Harvardian, another man shouts from the back, 'You one of them African niggas living large at Harvard on mah tax dollar when I cain't even afford mah next meal!'

The speaker shoots up from his seat. Now he is fighting his way forward, pushing past the people standing in the aisle. 'Outa my way, y'all, outa my fucking way!'

His big arms are like oars wading through a resistant body of water.

'Outa my way, y'all. Don't you hear me, outa my way.' Foaming at the mouth, the rhino on the rampage is bellowing, his dark face sweating. He cries again, 'I wanna get to that African nigga shit. Living large on mah tax dollar. You cain't get away now, conceited piece-a-shit. I'm a whup yo ass so bad you regret being born. It wasn't enough that you motherfuckers from Africa sold our forefathers into slavery, now you living large on our sweat . . .'

Vusi's African gods are on his side. The bus has arrived at Central Square where he has to get off anyway. He scrambles out with due haste.

Queenface

I

Queenface is squatting behind a bush, away from prying eyes. Flies are already buzzing about, impatiently waiting for her to finish her business so they can take over. Nature must run its course. Her eyes are full of fatigue, drooping. The sudden appearance of a quivering smudge on the northern horizon startles her to alertness. She uses her hand as a visor against the sun.

Is that a storm approaching?

She must get out of here. She shoots to her feet. Wait, she hasn't wiped. She squats again. No toilet paper, so she gathers a fistful of dried tree leaves, wipes her behind.

Her threadbare yellow pinafore billows in the afternoon air as she runs, at full tilt, towards her colleagues at the extreme end of the tobacco field. Tap-tap-tap-tap. Her bare feet on the hard-baked earth. She has to sound the clarion call. They have to run for cover. Only four weeks ago, almost the entire work-force at one of the neighbouring farms perished in a freak thunderstorm. Struck by lightning while they cowered under a clump of trees.

Her first thought is of her sister. She has to get Perseverance to safety. Her nieces are still at school, so they will be sheltered.

After a while, she slows down to a steady trot. Checks the

sky. It is placid. 'I'm being silly,' she says out loud, giggling. 'They are going to laugh at me.'

'My dear, why are you . . . carrying on . . . like a madwoman?'

She whirls around. Sees the owner of the voice bending over to rest the guitar he's been carrying on the ground, leaning on its neck, breathless. Shrieks at him: 'Magwegwe, you know it is a punishable offence on this farm to spy on women while they are doing their toilet?' She picks up a stone, throws it at him, misses.

'You know I can't let you out of my sight, my dear Queen-face.' It's clear he's been running behind her. 'There are monsters prowling the land, preying on old maids who refuse to get married even as wrinkles are beginning to assail their faces. My Queenface, I've loved you since we were children. But you already know that. Yet you won't find room for me in your big heart. Nevertheless, I won't stop protecting you. I won't stop running after you with my tongue hanging out of my mouth.'

'Magwegwe, go find yourself another woman. Forget about me.'

'Oh, just because I'm not educated like you? But how has your education helped you? You're working here on the farm like us uneducated people. Mugabe's economy does not discriminate. It cripples both the educated and uneducated.'

She digs into the pocket of her pinafore. Comes up with a piece of dried meat. She breaks it in two.

'Well,' Magwegwe says, gnawing at the tough piece of meat, 'even though our people say a dog with a bone in its mouth does not bark, you're not going to silence me with this. I'm not the type that gives up easily either.' He chews. 'I don't even mind you didn't wash your hands before you gave me this piece of meat. I'll fall sick when you do, and die where you die.'

'Shut up, you bowlegged freak. I'm still trying to collect my thoughts.' She looks up at the sky again, scratching her temple. 'For a moment I thought there was a storm coming.'

'I know you don't hate me; it's just that your heart is in chains. It is weighed down by shackles of doubt and distrust. Free your heart, my dear, so it can love me.'

'Look, Magwegwe, I love you as a brother—'

'Enough of that! Am I not man enough for you?'

'It's not that.'

'Then what is it?'

'Magwegwe, I'll be blunt with you for the first time. Look at you – you are young and able-bodied. Yet you are stuck here, with all these old people. Men your age are out there in South Africa. In Europe, in America, trying to eke out a proper living—'

'You too are young – girls your age are also out there in the countries you've mentioned.'

'My case is different.'

'Nonsense!' He mutters an apology, realising how harsh his voice must sound. 'I'll tell you something: I've toyed with the idea of leaving, too. But every time I think about you, I think you might just change your mind and accept me.'

'You stayed here on account of me?' Queenface raises her eyebrows.

'What have I been telling you all these years?'

Queenface sighs. 'Then if you stayed here on account of me, you have no vision. You have no ambitions.'

'What the hell does that mean?'

'I am not the marriageable type.' She sticks a finger in the air. 'Mark you, I didn't say I am not the marrying type. I said I am not the marriageable type. If you married me, you'd be miserable.'

Magwegwe steps forwards. 'I am tired of begging. Today I'm not taking no for an answer. I want you for a wife, dammit! Once you've said yes, then I can go to South Africa, Europe, America – to the moon itself – to work and earn enough money to make you happy.'

'Magwegwe!'

'What?' He looks flustered.

'Breathe in!' Queenface commands.

'What?'

'I said: breathe in!'

Magwegwe frowns, shrugs, then breathes in.

'Now breathe out.'

He obeys.

She smiles. 'Good. You seem relaxed now. I want to tell you that this thing you call love that you say you have for me, this emotion you're investing in me, is going down an abyss. It shall never realise a profitable return. If I said I loved and was ready to marry you – or anybody for that matter – I'd be lying. I don't want to lie to you—'

'I'm not like that bastard who stole your love, impregnated your sister, then ran away.'

Queenface cringes, not wanting to be reminded of this history. 'I know, Magwegwe, you're a sweet brother. I like you, but we can never be lovers.'

'You know,' he sighs, 'I'm always fighting with people who say you're full of shit.'

'You don't think I'm full of it?'

'After your expulsion of those thick smelly turds just a few minutes ago, I can put my head on the block and say: "No, she is not full of shit!"'

She snorts, suppressing her laughter.

'I will tell them you are not full of shit, but Queenface, you're sick.'

'Say what?'

'You are sick, that's what's wrong with you.' He plucks the strings of his ubiquitous guitar, and sings,

> You're sick and I'm your medicine.
>
> You have a stomach ache, and I am the Epsom salts.
>
> You have a headache, and I am the Disprin.
>
> You're wilting under the unforgiving sun; I'm the umbrella.
>
> You're dying of thirst; I'm the calabash of cold mahewu.
>
> Your feet are chapped and bleeding, and I'm your rubber sandals.
>
> Your hands are calloused from field work; I am the Zambuk.
>
> Your behind is soiled; I'm the toilet paper.
>
> I'm the tick of the clock, and you are the tock of the clock.
>
> Together we can go tick-tock, tick-tock.
>
> Tick-tock, the clock is ticking; the grave is beckoning.
>
> Open up your heart, girl, for I'm here knocking, waiting . . .

When she's recovered from her laughter, she says, 'I might be unwell in my head, but look out there in the distance.' She's pointing towards the north. 'Something is *definitely* approaching. Maybe not a storm, but it's something we need to notify the others about.'

Magwegwe stops playing the guitar. He squints into the distance, and concentrates. 'You paranoid old maid, it's a mere dust devil.'

'Except it's been like that for the past few minutes! I know what a dust devil is. A dust devil is here now, gone in an instant. That thing that's approaching keeps growing. Look, look!' She shivers.

Magwegwe wraps his arm around her protectively. She doesn't resist. They are quiet, eyes trained on the horizon. Even Magwegwe, a seasoned cowherd and hunter, now has to agree that it is not a passing dust devil.

When he speaks again there is a tremor in his voice: 'Four, six horsemen approaching us at a furious pace. Haven't seen horses in these parts in a long time.'

'What?'

He squints some more. 'More horsemen.' After a longish pause, he adds, 'No, no, those are not horses. Those are trucks. Five huge trucks.'

He grabs her by the wrist. They start running towards the main house.

II

Two hours later, Queenface, Magwegwe and the entire work-force of Golden Meadows – approximately a hundred and eighty of them – are on their knees, their hands in the air, right there behind the massive mansion where their boss, Master Wilson, lives with his family. Men armed with rifles move haughtily in between the rows of farmworkers, kicking stones, raising small clouds of dust. Queenface can see that some of the women are sobbing quietly, including her sister, Perseverance, who is kneeling beside her. The men have their eyes downcast, in fear and shame.

Master Wilson's dogs – a Rhodesian ridgeback, a German shepherd and a Great Dane – are lying under a tree, their fur covered in ribbons of blood. Dead.

'Well, well, well,' murmurs the man who appears to be in charge of the bandits, 'Golden Meadows. Everything here glitters like gold.' He takes a long drag from his cigar. He narrows his eyes as he exhales the smoke. Then he turns to one of his friends.

'Comrade Major-General,' one of his men says, 'those cars in the garage over there . . . if you give me that Range Rover, I'll declare the war over!'

The bandits laugh. The man in charge says, 'But, comrade, what have I been teaching you? Vision, vision! You take that car and where are you going to drive it? Have you seen the state the roads are in? And, there's no petrol in the land! The bloody imperialists have made sure of that.' His face darkens. In a harsh voice, he says, 'In other words, the cars, beautiful as they are, are the least of my concerns.'

When he stamps his foot on the ground, his men stand to attention.

'At ease!'

The men relax. He paces up and down, takes out his gun, looks at it absent-mindedly, puts it back into its holster.

'Golden Meadows,' he mutters to himself. 'Ah, to take ownership of Golden Meadows.'

With the exception of Queenface and maybe two or three others in the rest of Matabeleland, locals believe Master Wilson to be the owner of Golden Meadows, one of the most successful tobacco estates in Matabeleland. In truth, however, the owner is Hillary Walker, a billionaire businessman with interests in the copper mines of Zambia, the gold mines of South Africa and Australia, and money invested in various businesses and properties in France, the United States and Hong Kong. He hardly ever visits his farms in South Africa and Zimbabwe. Sir Hillary allows his employee Wilson so much leeway that the latter has even designed the main house on the farm to his own tastes. He lives like a true baron, Zimbabwe style. There are troops of uniformed servants buzzing about the house, cooking, cleaning, serving him tea and cucumber sandwiches at noon, and gin and tonic in the afternoon. He owns a collection of vintage and modern luxury cars. His wife flies regularly on social visits to South Africa and England.

Today, Master Wilson, with his wrists shackled behind his back, does not look regal at all. His upper lip is broken. A thread of blood trickles out of his nostril. Mrs Wilson, sitting on an upturned drum, with her hands shackled behind her, is staring at the dusty ground as if she can't bear to look at the marauders who have injured her husband. They are armed to the hilt. Menace is written on their ragged camouflage uniforms. It shoots from their eyes.

The man who appears to be in charge says, 'Master Wilson, we've heard all about you and how you run the farm . . .'

'Please, sir,' whines Master Wilson, 'I do not own this farm. I only run it on behalf of a very important man. If I were you I'd be careful—'

'We know this farm is owned by Sir Hillary,' says the man. He is of medium height, light in complexion, with eyes that are grey to the point of being almost the colour of water. 'In fact, Master Wilson, I've had occasion to drink cognac with Sir Hillary. Although a man of Empire through and through, he is intrinsically a good man, a good human being. His only fault is that he does not take note of the working conditions on his farms in South Africa and Zimbabwe. But you, Master Wilson, are an incorrigible bastard. Some of us have known you from childhood.' He pauses, looks deep into Master Wilson's eyes. Then he says, 'Ah, I'm jumping the gun here. I haven't even introduced myself. I am Major-General Chenjerai. These here are my comrades,' he says, sweeping his hand across the men armed with a variety of weapons ranging from AK-47s to Uzis and other guns that Queenface has never seen before. 'Master Wilson, we are the War Veterans. I'm sure you've heard of us.'

Indeed, everyone has heard of the War Veterans. But the War Veterans, as far as everyone knows, are a northern phenomenon. Bloodthirsty marauders who go around the country, taking over white-owned farms, raping women, pillaging. But these men – some of them too young to have fought during the war of the late 1970s – look so ordinary, Queenface observes, so down to earth. They look like somebody's son, somebody's uncle. No, these men are ordinary folk who seem to have fallen on hard times. Only their eyes – sharp, piercing, alert – betray an inner pain, an inner anger, a hunger for some unfulfilled dream. But they smile easily, occasionally joking with the farmworkers who stand respectfully in front of them – away from Master Wilson, who is rooted under a huge baobab tree.

'Queenie!' Master Wilson croaks, turning his attention to Queenface. 'Tell them we are the good guys. Tell them how we always play fair with you people.'

Queenface keeps staring at the dusty ground.

The air is rancid with Master Wilson's fear. He continues, 'Queenie, I know you can talk sense to them.'

'Shut up, Master Wilson!' screams Queenface. 'Face these soldiers like a man. Where are your balls? They are going to kill us all anyway. Make peace with that!'

Everybody seems startled by her outburst. Major-General Chenjerai looks her up and down. Then he says, 'So, beautiful one, are you the boss's girl? I think we'll make a soldier out of you.'

Queenface stares at him unblinkingly. A defiant idea starts jumping in her head. She grabs it by its tiny throat, wrestles it to the ground and strangles it before it becomes a fully fledged thought, before it becomes an utterance she might regret.

Around her, the other women's apprehension is palpable. They know Queenface has a sharp tongue. A careless tongue. They are always telling Queenface never to look a man in the eye. Especially not a man in authority.

Look away, look away, look away, don't say anything disrespectful, she can almost hear their thoughts. *Don't look at him. Look away, look away, he's dangerous, look away . . .*

But it is the major-general who looks away first. He turns his attention to the rest of the workers in front of him: 'My fellow black people, I have no issue with you. All I require of you is calm. Co-operate with us, and you will live to tell these tales to your children's children. You shall be heroes of the Third Chimurenga, the third revolution. But if you do not co-operate . . . we know every revolution has its casualties. We know what happened during the war against the white man. Our parents, friends, brothers, sisters perished like flies.'

Queenface's anger has subsided. She hasn't stopped looking at the soldier, at the sheen of his black military beret, his neat moustache that is so thin, it seems to be pencilled onto his skin.

Against her better judgment, she finds herself taken by his display of power, his purpose. His grey eyes turn her way again and seem to be staring at her. She thinks she can see herself in those eyes. They are that luminescent, almost like mirrors. If only she were not so powerless in this situation.

'Friends, we are here to ensure that this country does not have another Gukurahundi,' the man continues.

The mention of Gukurahundi hurls Queenface's mind back to the past.

III

Four years after her country achieved its independence, Mugabe's Shona people descended on Matabeleland. They were bent on decimating their Ndebele-speaking countrymen – or driving them across the border back to KwaZulu, from where they had originated during King Shaka Zulu's times. Queenface's eldest brother, Maxwell, whom she never got to know, had disappeared in the late 1970s to join the guerrillas fighting against Ian Smith's white racist regime. While the families of those whose sons had gone to fight against Smith celebrated the victorious return of their sons in 1980, the year the country gained independence, Queenface's family scanned the horizons endlessly, feeding their hearts with the hope of his appearance. But he never did appear.

By the time Mugabe and his soldiers descended on the Ndebele people, the family had long made peace with the fact that Maxwell had gone to the land of the ancestors. At the height of the anti-Ndebele genocide, her two other brothers disappeared. Her parents seemed to take solace in the fact that the unexplained disappearances were not exclusive to them. Such disappearances had become the norm. Funerals had also become the norm. Almost every weekend, three, four people from adjoining villages would be buried. Most of them would have died young. They would have died violently.

In typical African tradition, a funeral was preceded by a vigil the night before. One night, Queenface, aged ten, and her little sister, aged six, reluctantly joined their parents in attending one such vigil in the neighbourhood. Those days, the family lived not on a white-owned farm but in the communal lands. The move to Golden Meadows would come later.

It was a regular vigil – a lot of singing, preaching and testimonies from friends and neighbours about the dearly departed. By midnight, the singing had lost its earlier vigour. Queenface was missing her bed. Her sister had fallen asleep on a bench against the side of the marquee. All that was keeping Queenface there was that she was loath to wake little Perseverance and scared to walk home all by herself. So she stayed put, snoozing on the bench next to her sister and stealing snatches of sleep.

She was awoken by the urgent barking of dogs outside. She sat up. There was a lull. Then all of a sudden, the dogs started howling, one after the other, as if someone was beating them. Her sister, now awake, started to cry. The marquee they were sitting in exploded with gunfire. The paraffin lamp was knocked off its perch, plunging the interior of the tent into an inky darkness. Queenface cowered into a corner, hugging her sister close, wondering if she'd been shot. Wondering if she was already dead. Would she die at only ten years of age?

She covered her sister's body with her own, heard noises all around: the slurping sound made by the machetes as they drank blood; the shrieks and screams and moans and groans of people as their skulls succumbed to sticks and clubs. Silence followed. A number of bodies had piled on top of her and her sister. She could hardly breathe. She waited. With somebody's blood dripping into her face, she heard one or two of the attackers moving about. It was too dark to see. Just as well. She didn't want to see.

A disembodied voice spoke in a cool, relaxed manner: 'That snake is still alive, comrade. Clobber the snake. Chop that head.'

'Shine your torch, man; I can't see.'

Queenface shivered at the sound that followed, the noise that reminded her of her father using a machete to break open one of the big pumpkins their garden was blessed with.

The night swallowed the marauders. Their cries of triumph faded into the distance. Queenface shifted slightly under the weight of the corpses on top of her. She felt her sister shivering all over. A dog howled in the distance.

IV

Major-General Chenjerai is speaking again: 'The past is mercifully behind us. We are nowadays rebuilding the country. But we can't build on a shaky foundation. We have to sweep the dirt out of our way, reclaim what is rightfully ours. As President Mugabe correctly points out, we gave America and Britain thirty years to live up to the promises they made in the Lancaster House Agreement. They reneged on their promises to fund our land reform programme. Hence our campaign to reclaim the land by all means necessary . . .'

Queenface listens as one of the soldiers breaks into a popular liberation song, a Ndebele-language rendition of it. It's so infectious that even the farmworkers – some of whom probably soiled their pants at the appearance of the armed War Veterans – are now swimming in this river of music. The song rekindles memories of the war against Smith and his British running dogs.

There is a look of disbelief on Master Wilson's face as his own workers start singing and dancing alongside the veterans.

Major-General Chenjerai fires a burst of gunfire into the air. Some of his comrades follow suit. Then he lays his AK-47 on top of a makeshift table next to him. The singing climbs to a frenzied crescendo. The farmworkers' feet are thudding on the ground, sending swirls of dust into the air.

Finally, Major-General Chenjerai, who himself has been singing and dancing with careless abandon, raises his hands. The song fades away. There is a smile of contentment on his face. 'Ah, that's the spirit, my friends. I am happy you still re-member our liberation songs, chants that sustained us while we braved enemy bullets during those dark days. We come here in peace. We come here bearing revolutionary greetings from the rest of Zimbabwe. We come here to correct the distortions that have been created about us War Veterans by the Western imperialist media. You've been toiling on this farm all your lives so Sir Hillary can fly around in expensive jets; so Master Wilson here can afford to send his sons Trevor and William to Eton . . .'

Mrs Wilson's eyes grow big and round at the mention of her children.

'. . . so Mrs Wilson here can have high tea with Dame Cart-wright in England, and frequent the best shops in Paris and Johannesburg. Yes, some of the blame must go to Comrade Mugabe. He was too trusting. His blind commitment to this thing they call national reconciliation has come to bite him in the ass. It's thirty-three years after liberation, and the economy is in the doldrums. Now everyone is blaming Comrade Mugabe who, essentially, is the naïve do-gooder. The West has reduced him into a bogeyman, a raving lunatic. Because the West could not live up to their promises, Mugabe found he did not have money to even pay us our pensions, for services rendered during the War of Liberation. We had to start fending for ourselves. We had to take the war directly to the white farmers who have enjoyed the protection of the West. Intrinsically, we have nothing against white people, but through our actions we want to send a message to the Western world. The message is clear: southern Africa will not know peace until the West pays us reparations. We the War Veterans are going to turn things around.'

He pauses, looks at the workers, stretches out his arms to them with the palms of his hands facing up. 'As a way of turning things around, we must show our sense of goodwill to you, my people. Charity begins at home, after all. You've been working so hard, for so long. Now is the time for you to rest. To rest to your hearts' content. It's the time to eat as much as you can, before we escalate the revolution to another level. The unbroken song of your slavery has come to an end. We are taking you to the Promised Land. We have to move on to bigger things. Pamberi ne Chimurenga!'

'Pamberi,' the War Veterans *and* the farmworkers echo the cry, punching the air with their angry fists.

'Now you, comrade,' Major-General Chenjerai points at Magwegwe, 'yes, you with the guitar, you with the bowlegs. I want you to tie Master Wilson to that tree. Yes, you!' He points to two more farmworkers. 'And you and you. Help Mr Bow-legged Fellow to tie Master Wilson up to that tree.'

One of the soldiers relieves Magwegwe of his guitar.

The men who have been pointed out to join Magwegwe baulk, each man pushing the other forward. 'The big soldier pointed at you, not me!'

One of the veterans shoots a burst of gunfire at the hesitant men's feet. The men scurry towards Master Wilson.

Queenface steals a glance at Master Wilson. The master's eyes have in them the restless agony of impotence in search of sympathy. Then she looks at Magwegwe. She stares straight into his eyes. Next to her, Perseverance, too, is looking at Magwegwe.

Magwegwe clears his throat, says, 'Comrade Soldier Sir, we don't know how to tie him to the tree . . .' Queenface knows he is in effect saying, *Master Wilson, it's not my fault that these indignities should be visited upon you.*

But Major-General Chenjerai will not co-operate in Magwegwe's exoneration. An edge to his voice, he says, 'Oh yes, you do know how to tie him up! Tie him the way a dyed-in-the-wool Rhodesian farmer would tie up his wayward worker before he flogs him. You know exactly how to do it. Unless you want me to come over there and remind you . . .'

Within minutes, Master Wilson has been stripped down to his underpants. He is dangling by his ankles, from a strong tree branch.

'Are you enjoying your upside-down view of the world now, Master Wilson?' one soldier says, laughing at his own joke.

Major-General Chenjerai then turns to the women gathered in a small group. 'Now, you two ladies over there, tie Missus Wilson against that pole. I don't want people to think we are discriminating against women. Women are part of our struggle. Tie her the way they would tie an errant female worker.'

Ably guided by Magwegwe, four women manage to tie Missus Wilson with her back against a pole.

'Now,' continues Major-General Chenjerai, 'after all that hard work, Mr Bowlegged Man, isn't your throat parched? And don't you feel, er, peckish?'

'I guess so, baas . . .' Magwegwe stares at his feet.

'I'm not your fucking boss!' thunders Major-General Chenjerai.

Magwegwe fumbles his hands together. 'Sorry, Major-General Commander Comrade, I am not used to military ranks. How do you want me to help? Always at your service, sir.'

Queenface looks at Magwegwe in sheer disgust. *He wants my hand in marriage, grovelling like a dog in front of another man. I am not asking him to get himself killed, but if he has to co-operate with them, he must do so with dignity.*

Magwegwe avoids her eyes as he and four other men are led away by the major-general and three of his underlings. A few minutes later, they come back, leading a big Friesland cow.

'Tether it to that tree,' says Major-General. 'I want you to slaughter it in front of Master Wilson.'

Master Wilson, who seemed to be succumbing to vertigo, is startled back to alertness at the mention of his name. From his upside-down vantage point, he looks on as Lady Antoinette, his favourite cow, is tied to a tree close by.

'Whatever you do,' he croaks, a touch of arrogance creeping back into his voice, 'whatever you do, you can't hurt Lady Antoinette. She's the best producer of milk in the entire region. If it is meat you want to eat, go to Verwoerd over there. He's the Bonsmara bull I've been fattening up for the market. He'll yield enough beef to feed the entire continent for a month. Don't touch Lady Antoinette.'

'Shut up, Bill!' Mrs Wilson screams, jolting everyone's attention.

One soldier cocks his gun, and says, 'Hey, Mr Bowlegged Man, what's your name?'

'You've just said it, sir: I am Magwegwe, the bowlegged one.'

'That's your true name?'

'My grandfather gave it to me.'

'Okay, Magwegwe, move over so I can shoot the cow.'

'No, no, no!' says Major-General Chenjerai. 'I want Magwegwe to slaughter the beast the proper way. The traditional way. Two soldiers must escort Magwegwe to his compound so he can retrieve a spear to slaughter this animal. We must do things the proper way, soldier. We are not in the bush here. We are in the company of civilised people. And we are offering this cow as a sacrifice to the gods of the revolution. Pamberi ne Chimurenga!'

'Pamberi!' the other soldiers chorus.

A few minutes later, Magwegwe and the two soldiers are back. With just one thrust of his spear to the heart, Magwegwe brings the cow to the ground. It bellows. Mrs Wilson faints. The soldiers cheer and fire their guns to celebrate that the cow has bellowed, a good omen. The gods of the revolution are smiling their benevolence upon the proceedings.

Master Wilson's eyes are closed. He hangs limply. He does not appear conscious most of the time. Now and then his eyelids open slightly. His male workers sing and chat as they happily skin his best milk producer. The women are preparing various fires where the meat will be cooked once it has been quartered. Even Josephine, the housemaid who always thinks of herself as superior to common farmworkers, has got off her high horse. Unprompted, she scurries to the kitchen and returns with spices.

The mood is festive, a change of pace for everyone. Magwegwe has his guitar back. He is plucking the strings and singing, making everyone laugh. That's how they know him: the ugly, bowlegged guitar wizard. Even Master Wilson has always allowed Magwegwe to take the guitar with him wherever he goes. When the sun was hot in the tobacco fields, and the workers sluggish, Master Wilson would instruct Magwegwe to play one of his inspirational songs. A song that would make them laugh. A song that would get those fingers working nimbly on the tobacco leaves. A work song.

To Queenface, life at Golden Meadows has always been one monotonous, unbroken song of work, work, work. Five days a week, week after week, month after month, year after year. Work, work, work. Even school-going children would have to perform a few chores – milking cows, chopping wood, feeding pigs and chickens – before rushing off to the farm school. There, Queenface's nieces have told her, in between lessons about mitosis, chromosomes, dolomitic soil, Cecil John Rhodes, Robert Mugabe and Jesus Christ, they would also be reminded about the virtues of less talk, less complaining and more work, work, work. And then after school, the children would join their parents in the tobacco fields where hoes and shovels would make love to the soil. Work, work, work.

On Saturdays the workers would go to church (all of them are Seventh Day Adventists), and on Sundays they would stay at home – the mothers mending their children's school uniforms, the men hammering away at broken benches or tending their own small, private vegetable patches which Master Wilson grudgingly allowed them to keep. Some would visit friends and relatives on neighbouring farms where they would gossip about their respective bosses. They would share news about sons, daughters or relatives who have left Zimbabwe for the supposedly greener patches of grass in South Africa, America, the United Kingdom, or Canada. They would speak in hushed tones about those who'd fallen foul of Mugabe's security police. Some of these are dead. The lucky ones are in Chikurubi and other prisons.

When the sun began to recede behind the mountains on the last day of the weekend, they would say their goodbyes. Like rabbits they would skitter down the village footpaths, the twilight shadows snapping at their heels like keen dogs. They had to be in bed soonest. For the following day, the song of their lives would have to resume: work, work, work.

But that was the Golden Meadows of a few weeks ago, of a few days ago, of yesterday. Today is a different day at the farm.

A truck comes trundling down the road leading to the farm. Queenface squints to see, wondering what new fate will befall them. When the truck stops at Master Wilson's house, soldiers jump out of the front, and salute Major-General Chenjerai. Then they go round the back of the truck and open the doors. Children poor out. There are about twenty of them – children of the farmworkers who had been in school. The teachers are also there. Queenface's heart starts hammering when she sees her nieces, Nomfundo and Nozizwe. Some of the children are crying, and the soldiers shout at them to stop.

'The children must go to that storage facility,' Major-General

Chenjerai says to the soldiers. 'You must guard over them. It is for their own good.'

With the armed soldiers looming over them, parents are given a chance to hug their children. Queenface's nieces come bounding towards their mother. Nomfundo, the eldest at sixteen, is crying. Nozizwe, fourteen years of age, is quiet. The look in her eyes is as sharp as the spear that felled Lady Antoinette. She buries her head in her mother's bosom very briefly. Then she goes over to Queenface and her face relaxes a little. They regard each other for a while, before they embrace.

'It will soon be over,' Perseverance says to the children.

'Why are you lying to them?' says Queenface. 'We don't even know what's happening. How then can we guess when it will be over?' She turns to Nozizwe and Nomfundo. 'Girls, from now on we are going to have to be very strong. Each one of us has to look out for the others. We have no idea what is happening.'

They only have time for one more hug before the children are all led away.

Perseverance turns on Queenface. 'Why are you always driving a wedge between me and my children?' she hisses.

'Just telling them the truth, sis.'

'It's your domineering ways that drive men away from you. No man will tolerate this nonsense of yours.'

'You want to tell me about men? Where is that thing of yours you call a man? Isn't he the one who made you a laughing stock in this region, fucking everything that moves?' Queenface clicks her tongue. 'You want to tell me about men.'

'You are just jealous he didn't choose you . . .'

'Choose me?' she sniggers. 'So he chose you. And the whores

61

out there chose him in turn. He's out there impregnating women as if it were going out of fashion. It's a pity donkeys and cows can't talk, otherwise they would have told us stories about him too. He fucks everything.' She shakes her head. 'The one who chose you. Where's the coward now? Tell me where is he?'

'Shh,' an elderly woman hisses at them. 'Stop fighting, will you? You're going to make these soldiers angry!'

The other women are shaking their heads sadly, throwing accusing glances at the two sisters. Queenface walks a few paces away, turns her back on them. She hears one of them say, 'After all these years, the old spinster is still jealous that her boyfriend decided to marry the younger sister.'

The next one joins in: 'And gave her beautiful children too.'

'Beautiful and intelligent.'

'But the younger girl seems to be taking after her aunt. Always arguing with boys.'

'Yes, she is behaving like a boy. Even tries to speak like a boy.'

'She doesn't even have hips. Flat-chested, too.'

'Ah, women, you're being unfair now,' says a new voice. 'She is but a child. Thirteen or fourteen.'

'Hey, wena, are you walking around with your eyes closed? Girls her age have ample hips and huge melons are jiggling from their chests.'

'But everyone is different. Give her a year or two – she will be having respectable mounds on her chest.'

'At this rate, I doubt it. She is willing herself not to develop and mature into a woman.'

'Are you saying she wants to be one of these sexless creatures?'

Queenface feels the anger building up inside her but she refuses to turn around. She will not be provoked. She will not get sucked into these ignorant women's gossiping. She pretends to busy herself looking for sticks for the cooking fires.

'Please, my neighbour,' she hears, 'do not speak of the sexless ones in my presence. They drive the fear of God into my heart. Remember, my man is out there in Kimberley and we have yet to have a child. What if our first-born turns out to be a boy who is a girl, or a girl who is a boy? I am so scared, people, of this malady afflicting the land.'

Unobtrusively, Queenface glances at the gossipers. An older woman, wearing a blue pinafore, speaks for the first time: 'Relax, my dear, you're a God-fearing daughter of the soil. Such misfortune will never befall you. Only Godless people will beget homosexuals.'

'But I know a good, God-fearing woman whose son is one of them,' a woman of considerable girth is saying. 'Why am I being coy? My sister in Harare has a son who counts himself in the ranks of the sexless ones.'

'What do you expect, my daughter?' says Blue Pinafore. 'She is living among those Godless Shona people. You see, I'll teach you something: in the Good Book we first learn of homosexuals in the story of Sodom and Gomorrah. Why? Because people of those towns had sinned against God. And he punished them. Simple and straightforward. If you bear a homosexual child, it means you might have transgressed, and God is punishing you. But don't fret. Our God is graceful. He will forgive you and your evil spawn, as long as you confess your sins in public and proclaim your love of Jesus Christ!'

Queenface turns away in disgust.

'But, mother,' she hears a voice say, 'even the educated doctors say homosexuality can be explained medically.'

'It is because the so-called educated doctors of yours are in the service of the Evil One!'

Someone jumps in: 'Perseverance's girl is surely one of the sexless ones. No hips, no breasts. You were right, my sister. I think, like her aunt who has no child and no man in her life, this girl is one of the sexless creatures.'

'This girl is dangerous. She won't even play with other girls.'

'Quiet and aloof like her aunt.'

'Two peacocks in a pod!'

'It's our duty to make her a woman. We should get one of the bigger boys to deal with her. Take her to the sack and teach her a lesson. She is a little mare that needs to be broken. That's all. A good dick will go a long way towards curing her.'

Queenface can hear the merriment in the woman's tone, but she is not amused. 'Stupid bitches,' she mutters to herself.

A group of women close to the gossipers beckon to Queenface to come help them to clean pots. She goes over to them, straining her ears to hear what is being said about her, her sister and nieces. But in her own group of pot cleaners, a different conversation is going on:

'It's all thanks to Mugabe that we're at the mercy of these so-called War Veterans. Why can't he just keel over and die?' a young woman with a small pregnant belly is saying.

'Any guarantees that the next ruler will be any better?' Queenface offers.

'Maybe that slut of his can take over. Grace is her name.'

'Interesting point. She could be the first female president. Power to the women.'

'Slut?!' a wrinkled old woman in their group says, aghast. 'Just tell me: who is the father of her children?' She answers her own question: 'Mugabe, of course!'

'But can he still make the cock crow?' Queenface jibes.

The younger woman bursts out laughing. When she has sufficiently recovered, she says, 'But, the white man has brought us blue pills, pink pills and all kinds of pills to make up for our flagging appetites in pursuits of a physical nature. Thanks to one of these pills, a man of ninety can still make the cock crow. Endlessly.'

'I won't be surprised if those Mugabe children turn out to be homosexual and evil,' the older woman says. 'They were conceived the wrong way, with the aid of evil pills. Anyway, why are you girls so full of laughter while the vultures are circling us?'

'Well, mama, in Africa we laugh even in time of death.'

'To be honest,' another woman in the group adds, 'I don't think these veterans are going to kill us. They came here to raid Master Wilson's cupboards. Have you noticed how much they have been eating of the master's expensive food, and quaffing his expensive beers and things? I think they are here because they are hungry.'

The pot Queenface is cleaning is already shiny. She can see her frowning face reflected. These women are all so naïve.

The soldiers, though still armed and alert, seem more relaxed now. They walk about, monitoring the cooking of food. Every now and then, a soldier's stray hand spanks a woman's backside. The women are too relaxed; they do not seem to mind. The younger ones even have the courage to tease the soldiers: 'You men with guns have been making love to your guns in the bush for so long. Do you still know how to handle the warmth of a woman?'

Queenface's agitation is rising. She clenches her fists. She wants to scream into these women's faces: *Why don't you open those legs and be done with it once and for all? We've just been kidnapped. We should be putting our heads together, coming up with a plan. These fuckers, like all men who think they are in charge, are not in charge. They've never done this before. Breast-beating adventure seekers who lack resolution. Bitches, let's get together, come up with a plan!*

Snatches of the gossipers' conversation behind her reach her ears again.

'But where is that man, by the way, the father of Perseverance's miserable children?' one says. 'A crying shame, leaving a woman with such beautiful children. How can she cope by herself?'

'No elephant has ever complained about the heaviness of its trunk.'

'True that, true that. But what really happened to the husband? Why did he suddenly take off?'

'He fell for the lure of a more strong-willed mistress . . .'

'You're talking nonsense. That man has always had women at his beck and call, but that never separated him from his family.'

'No, the new mistress was music.'

'You're speaking in riddles, girl.'

'Joined a music band from Harare. And together they fled to South Africa, then the UK. And I hear they are now in Canada.'

'I've always maintained that this modern music of drums and guitars would be the undoing of the civilised black community. Modern music is a sin. The alchemy of evil.'

'Yes, the devil uses music as a passage into the hearts of unsuspecting people. And before they know it, they have stopped believing in God . . .'

'Just like this man who's abandoned his children to worship at the shrine of the devilish whore called modern music.'

'To show that this is the devil's work, the band he has joined is led by a Shona man.'

'After what the evil Shonas did to us!'

'The devil works in mysterious ways.'

Queenface has had enough. She gets up and turns towards them.

V

At her approach, they shrink back. She comes to an abrupt stand, suddenly self-conscious. She is breathing heavily, her nostrils flared, her chest rising and falling.

She wants to drag them by their hair across the dusty yard.

She wants to drag them by their titties and kick their fat asses.

She wants to pummel them until they shit, and force them to eat their shit.

Tears suddenly flood her eyes. They come out in torrents, burning her cheeks. Through her tears she can see her sister Perseverance standing some distance away, quartering meat, stealing glances at her.

Perseverance, who Queenface had protected with her own body when they were children. Perseverance, who did not hesitate to embrace the man who had failed to force Queenface to fall pregnant. Perseverance, who did not follow her sister's logic: let's finish school, get a bursary, go to university, start working, and then we can start having babies.

Perseverance, who, in this huge forest called life, a paradise with an abundance of trees of possibility and opportunity, decided to single out the tree of misery. To embrace it. To water it with her tears of defeat. To feed it with the manure of sadness.

Perseverance, who sat patiently through her elder sister's pep talks about freedom and responsibility. Talks about vision, about planning. Talks about life.

'Percy, look at me!' she used to say.

'But I am.'

'I'm saying it figuratively, silly. I mean, look at what I do; how I conduct my affairs; how I carry myself . . .'

'You're successful at getting people to talk: you carry yourself like a man; you drink with men.'

'Exactly my point. If you go through life wondering, *What will people say?*, you will not get anywhere; you will not live! I don't care what they say about me. Some say I am a slut. Others say I sleep with other women, that's why I don't have a man. But they will never point out one single woman and say: she is the one who sleeps with Queenface . . .'

'Still, they talk.'

'What should I do to stop them talking?'

'Modify your behaviour. Behave like a . . . like a normal woman.'

She used to force herself to breathe when her sister said such things.

'Percy, Percy,' she'd say. 'You mustn't fear what others say about you. You will never satisfy people. You should hear what they are saying about you—'

'What are they saying, what are they saying?'

'Doesn't matter.'

'To me it does.'

'Okay, suit yourself: they say you are lazy. Other girls your age have not stopped with their studies—'

'You're lying. People around here do not care that much about education. You yourself have said it sometimes. People with degrees in Bulawayo and Harare are sitting at home because they can't find work. You yourself said it!'

'I don't know if I said that. If I did, maybe I was saying people must be careful what degree they take at university, if it is relevant to our current situation . . .'

Perseverance would pull a face. 'You're always playing with my mind. You're always changing things, twisting me around in the head.'

'Your problem, little sister, is that you allow fear to rule you. Look, fear might paralyse you for a moment. We all have moments of anxiety, moments of self-doubt. But that's what they are: moments. We cannot let them consume our lives. A life is bigger than a moment. Fear is a moment. It can only run your life if you allow it to.'

'Big words, big words. All you're doing is trying to confuse me. I am not going to fall for your tricks. I have a man; you don't. I have children; you don't. I have love; you don't.'

'Fine, fine, little sister. All I am saying and what I have always said is simply this: live your life; I'll live mine. In fact, I'll put it this way: I don't allow life to happen to me. I happen to life. Did you get that?'

'What now?'

'I said: life does not happen to me. *I happen to it!*'

Indeed, from a young age, Queenface had the temerity to grab Life by its throat. Wrestled it to the ground. Squeezed its throat, until – spluttering and coughing, snot coming out of its nose – Life croaked, 'Okay, okay, time out. If you let go of my throat, I'll never poke my nose into your affairs. I'll just let you be.'

Life kept its promise to her. It let her be. Since then, Queenface has existed on planet Earth on her own terms. 'Life doesn't happen to me! I happen to it!' That's what she said to her younger sister when the latter politely asked her to find herself a man, settle down and take life seriously. Back then, Percy's life looked rosy: she had a man and two children.

'I don't care what these bitches think of me,' Queenface uttered to herself numerous times when everyone laughed at how her younger sister had stolen her man. 'I don't even care what my sister thinks of me. What I know is that I am stuck with my sister. The two of us are like those Siamese twins, stuck at the hip. If she goes this way, I have to go. If I go the other, she has to come. She can break the bond if she likes, but I will fight her to the death. Because I love her that much. I'll love her to death.'

Then Perseverance's man started impregnating women all over the place. This was before he went to South Africa, where he disappeared and was never to be heard from again.

When it became clear he was not coming back, and the children were growing up, Queenface never said to her sister, 'I told you so!'

Instead, she cancelled her own plans to move to Harare, where one of her friends had found her a secretarial job. She stayed with her sister. Perseverance had invested her hope in her marriage. With her husband gone, she was bound to go crazy. Imagine the two little children at the mercy of a crazy mother.

No schooling, no intellectual resource whatsoever, no survival skills.

The women of the farm started telling another story to explain the disappearance of her sister's husband: Queenface, in a fit of jealousy, had bewitched him. She had cast on him a spell called dukanezwe – disappear into the world. An infamous spell that would ensure that the man never came back home. If she couldn't have the man, her sister could not have him either.

That story is still in circulation to this day. Queenface wipes her tears at all these memories. She finds herself thinking about those beautiful children of her sister's. Especially Nozizwe. *That one is like my own daughter. She understands me even before I open my mouth. I can't let them down. I can't let her down.*

She thinks she has a plan to get them – at least her sister and her family – out of this. It won't be popular, she knows. But to her, life was never a popularity contest anyway.

It's a plan nevertheless.

VI

The following morning, Master Wilson is still hanging by his ankles from the tree. There's a puddle of vomit near him. Queenface comes strutting out of the main house, walking side by side with Major-General, as if they are a loving couple. It was not difficult to infiltrate his inner circle. He was looking at her with lust the whole of yesterday. When she started smiling at him, he quickly took the bait. Queenface has changed into a red dress from Mrs Wilson's wardrobe. Earlier, in the full-length mirror in the master bedroom, she saw that the dress accentuates her hips, and imprisons her breasts so that they look as if they are fighting hard to break free. She is wearing a pair of white trainers – also Mrs Wilson's. Her face is scrubbed. She has undone her cornrows. Her big soft hair has been greased properly. Combed back, and tied in a ponytail.

The women, already busy with the morning fires, raise their heads to look at her. They look at one another. Shake their heads. Click their tongues in irritation. Go back to their pots.

Major-General Chenjerai looks startled when he sees Master Wilson. He glances at Queenface, then looks towards three War Veterans sitting nearby. 'Comrades, the white man is still hanging from the tree? That's very inhumane. Did you feed him at least?'

Three War Veterans, their rifles resting next to them, look up from the breakfast they are eating. They look at Master Wilson. Look at their commander. Then look back at their food: a loaf of bread, a hunk of meat and a Castle beer.

'What are you waiting for?' bellows the senior officer. 'Your breakfast is not going to grow feet! Get up and untie that white man. Give him food. You women over there, help Mrs Wilson clean herself up. Come on, give her some food too. We are not monsters.'

Everyone is staring uncomprehendingly at the major-general.

Queenface says, 'What are you all looking at? You women get Mrs Wilson to the bathroom. Clean her up and get her some food. Fast. Off your fat asses. Come on.'

Major-General Chenjerai looks lovingly at her. Then he seems to remember that he is being watched. He coughs, stands up straight and scowls at his soldiers. 'Okay, everybody, eat your breakfast, clean yourselves up. Once you're done, I'll give you the schedule for the day. Come on, get moving. And you, troops, no beer drinking at this time!'

Queenface moves to where some of the farmworker women are preparing food. She nods to her sister, who looks at her worriedly. The other women sniff indignantly when she takes her place among them, but she ignores them. They have always thought her to be a slut; this is nothing new. They should thank her for giving them something real to gossip about.

As soon as the major-general's back is turned, Magwegwe joins Queenface where she is plucking a freshly killed chicken. 'Your sense of loyalty is admirable,' he sneers. 'Hardly a day with these dogs, you're now doing their bidding. Sleeping with their boss. Disgusting.'

'Use your brain. If you want to know what your enemy is thinking, bring him closer. Lull him into complacency.'

'Oh, yeah, Miss Educated Know-it-all. So what is on the enemy's mind?'

'We're leaving this farm tonight. All of us.'

'Where to?'

'Don't know exactly. But it sounds scary. We have to do something drastic—'

'Careful! He's coming.' Magwegwe melts behind the barn.

Late in the evening, with parcels of meat and some of their clothing packed in bags and flimsy suitcases, the farmworkers are made to stand in three lines: one for men, one for women, and the last one for children. Six soldiers are taking down the names of those in line into thick, hardcover books. Each person is then assigned a number. Once everyone's name has been entered into the book, a roll call is shouted: 'Magwegwe Ntuli, number 8!'

'Yes, sir.'

'Mangisi Moyo, number 3.'

'Yes, sir!'

At the end of the roll call, numbers and names are tallied. All is in order.

'Okay, soldiers,' says Major-General Chenjerai in his authoritative voice, 'let's get ready to go.'

'It's all systems go, sir. Everyone has taken some items of clothing and some food with them. They won't be needing a lot of that when we get to our destination anyway.'

'Good, soldier, yours is to do what I say, not to explain to me what's going to happen from here on.'

'Yes, sir, Comrade Major-General.'

A light breeze is blowing across the land. Hills and trees are squatting in the gathering darkness. The soldiers seem more fidgety now, moving rapidly up and down the three straight lines of people.

Some children are beginning to cry, 'Where are they taking us to?'

'Why are they leaving Master Wilson hanging from a tree like that?'

'I want to stand next to my mother . . .'

'Shut up, you little rat,' a soldier shouts at the boy who is crying for his mom.

'Easy, soldier, easy,' says Major-General Chenjerai, 'you don't want to scare the children now. You don't want to scare anyone.'

Now he raises his voice, addressing everyone: 'The time has now come to leave Golden Meadows. In order to protect you, we won't tell you where we're going. It should be a pleasant surprise. We've got all your names written down, and we will keep checking that everyone behaves, that everyone plays by the rules. You must always ask for permission if you want to go to the toilet. Always. Whatever you do, you don't do it unaccompanied by a soldier. Whatever you do. This is all to protect you. Now, soldiers, start the trucks.'

The drivers move towards the periphery of the yard. This is where the trucks are parked, hulking shapes, like the ruins of Great Zimbabwe in the darkness.

The Major-General continues: 'All of you are now going to be blindfolded. You are then going to be cuffed behind your backs, and then led to the trucks. Your possessions have already been loaded.'

'Maye-maye! Are we prisoners now?' one woman cries. 'Why the blindfolds? Why the handcuffs? Come on, you can't do this!'

A soldier advances on the woman, menacingly.

'Shut up, you fool!' Queenface speaks in a harsh voice.

'What? You?'

'You're being rescued from a life of hell,' says Queenface. 'And you are crying! Ungrateful piece of shit.' She looks at the major-general, who nods approvingly.

Magwegwe, plucking his guitar strings, starts singing,

> And so comes the night, when we bid Golden Meadows goodbye.
> 'Tis time to hit the road, not to sing our children a lullaby . . .

VII

By Queenface's estimation, it must be midnight. For hours now, the truck has been bouncing, clattering, rumbling along what feels like uneven, rutted dirt roads. Sometimes she gets the sense the trucks are fighting their way through uncharted territory, carving new paths through virgin bush. Blindfolded and her hands shackled behind her back, she is relying on her sense of sound and smell.

She had hoped that the major-general would not blindfold her along with all the others. That he would have perhaps let her ride in the front of the truck, but she was herded into the back with the rest of the farmworkers. He is infatuated – that much was evident during their lovemaking the previous night, but he does not yet trust her enough. She would have to up her game. She has to do it for her sister and for Nozizwe and Nomfundo. She hopes they are okay, somewhere in the darkness of the truck.

Queenface coughs repeatedly as dust rises to her nostrils. When she parts her lips, and tries to breathe through her mouth, a film of dust forms a thick coating on her tongue. She gathers a gob of saliva, and spits carelessly.

'Who's that spitting into my face?'

There's pushing and jostling. One of the soldiers screams, 'Shut up, you cow dung-smelling fucking peasants!'

Night air seems to accentuate the smells of nature. At intervals Queenface can perceive the mature odour of cow dung. And then there is the acrid smell of wildfires, burning grass.

They drive on. Every now and then someone breaks into a song; the others take it. But in due course, there's less vigour in the singing. Finally, the singing comes to a stop. All that can be heard now is the clattering sound of the truck as it bounces on rocks and ruts.

There's a sudden change in the air. She can smell dampness. There must be a river nearby. A man next to her – he has the tang of tobacco on his breath but the pungency of his armpits proclaims its dominion above all odours – says, 'Soldier man, where exactly are you sending us? Let us say our last prayers to the motherland before you kill us, at least. What have we done?'

Somebody breaks into the old struggle song: 'Senzeni Na, Senzeni Na?' – 'What have we done, what have we done? Our sin is our blackness, what have we done.'

'Shut up!' a soldier commands.

VIII

It is the sound of music that startles Queenface from her deep sleep. Ears pricked, she listens to the familiar melody. It comes to her in inspiring waves of staccato:

> Jerusalem city, the city of the Lord. Jerusalem city, the city of the Lord.
> I want to be there, I want to be there, to be the-rre-rree forever more!
> Forever mo-ho-ho. I want to be there, I want to be the-rre-rree forever more!

When she sits up, she remembers that she doesn't know where she is. She looks around. She realises she's sleeping on a mattress, which is on the floor, inside what seems to be a tent, judging by the low, sloping roof, no windows. This is the second-most comfortable bed she's ever slept in. The first was the double bed in Master Wilson's master bedroom, which she shared with the major-general two nights ago. At home she used to sleep on hard-packed earth covered with a goatskin, or a grass mat. The comfort offered by this bed atones for the uncomfortable thought that hit her when she woke up – the fact that she doesn't know where she is. As her eyes adjust to the darkness, she realises that the soldier is sitting on a chair facing her mattress, watching her intently.

'My angel is finally awake,' Major-General Chenjerai says quietly.

'Where are we? Where am I?'

'You're even more beautiful waking up. Not many people are comfortable with the idea of showing their faces to the public just as soon as they've woken up. But, you, you are an angel. My angel of the morning. Do you remember that song?' He clears his throat and sings in a falsetto, 'Just call me angel of the morning, just touch my cheek before you leave me, AAANGEL, AAAANGEL!'

He is on his feet now, naked, singing at the top of his voice in the falsetto. He is holding an imaginary microphone and stamping his feet with passion. His penis jiggles, slapping his thigh with a nasty sound as he jumps about, as if possessed.

'Just touch my cheek before you leave, angel, angel . . .'

Then, breathing heavily, he sits down on the chair again. For the first time, she notices the Bible on the floor next to his chair. Brownish powder has been sprinkled on the cover of the Bible. There are some banknotes on the floor next to the Bible. Now he kneels on the floor, picks up one of the banknotes. He shapes it into a tube. Bends over and starts inhaling the powder through the tube. Several times. Then he straightens up, throws his head back, and goes, 'Ah, that feels good.'

'What's that? What's that you're putting inside your nostrils? Aren't you going to choke?'

'It's my morning medicine, angel. Angel of the morning.' He starts singing again, 'Just call me angel of the morning, baby . . .'

He starts inhaling the powder. 'This is my feelgood medicine, darling. This is Dr Feelgood. Ever heard of Aretha Franklin? Beautiful sister from America. Got this voice as rich, thick and sweet as honey. Sings about a man who makes her feel good. Calls him Dr Feelgood. Yes, sweetheart, this is my Dr Feelgood, my morning medicine. Dr Feelgood in the morning.'

She looks intently at him. He is sounding like a child who's just been given a tub full of sweets. He is over-excited. His hands are flying all over. He says, 'Come, come get a feel of the medicine. You'll enjoy the feeling, the sensation. It will uplift. Yes, it is uplifting. Dr Feelgood.'

He picks up the Bible, and crawls across the floor to reach her. 'Here.' He thrusts the Bible into her face.

'No.'

'Please. Just once. Inhale just once, and see what happens. Do it for me, angel. My angel of the morning. My beautiful, wonderful angel of the morning.'

She shakes her head.

He frowns, grabs her arm, hard. 'Do it!'

Hands trembling, she accepts the banknote tube from him. She inserts it into her right nostril. Tears are welling in her eyes – tears of anger, of impotence. But she has to do what she's being told to do. She bends forwards. Inhales once. Straightens up. Looks at him, shrugs. 'I don't feel anything.'

He reaches out for a pouch, opens it and sprinkles its contents across the black cover of the Bible. 'Do it again, my girl. Inhale.'

She bends forward, inhales. She inhales again, and again. Sits up. Closes her eyes. She is feeling giddy. She begins to giggle. And she can't stop.

'What's this, Mr Soldier Man, what's this? What is it made of?'

'We call it "brown-brown", my dear girl. It's cocaine mixed with gunpowder. Always hits the target. Bam-bam.' He points a finger at her as if it were a gun. 'Bam-bam!'

She collapses onto the mattress, eyes tightly shut. For a while she remains in that position, transported to another world. Then slowly, ever so slowly, she opens her eyes. Her eyes are looking at the roof of the tent. She is smiling; her lips can't seem to close over her teeth. She has no control over strings of saliva dribbling from both corners of her mouth. He comes over and kisses her on the lips.

'How are you feeling all right?' he says.

She starts laughing. Repeating the words, 'How are you feeling all right? How are you feeling all right? Mr Soldier Man, are you high on something? What kind of speech is that? He says, how are you feeling all right? How are you feeling all right.'

She closes her eyes. She's floating and enjoying the sensation.

From somewhere, a little voice is telling her that she is meant to be on a mission. She is meant to be gathering information from the soldier. She giggles at the stern little voice. 'Mr Soldier Man,' she asks him, 'where are we? Are you going to tell me where we are? This brown-brown has hit the target. Bam-bam! You're naughty, Mr Soldier Man, you know that? You're cruel. But where are we?'

'At camp,' he says. 'Relax. Everything is in order. You were too tired to see or understand anything last night.'

'Of course I couldn't see anything with a blindfold on.'

She wants to say something, but he joins her underneath the covers. The brown-brown seems to have ignited an appetite in her. They start making love. It is different from the previous night when she was just pretending. She is hyper-aware of his body, the way his muscles move beneath her hands. She has lost all sense of control.

Afterwards, lying next to him, she becomes aware of music again. Singers outside. But she cannot identify the song.

Suddenly, he sits up and says, 'Fortune favours the brave and the reckless, I've heard it said. It did not make sense to me until now. Until I embarked upon this mission.'

'What mission?'

'This mission you're part of.'

'I'm not part of any mission.' She is trying to regain her self-control, her self-respect. *I'm doing this to gather information,* she tells herself. *I'm doing this for my sister and my nieces.* She looks at him. 'What I know is that I have been kidnapped, taken from my home against my will.'

'You haven't shown much resistance, have you?'

Heat rises to her face. 'I would have been killed had I tried to resist. You know that. I am not stupid.'

'You think you'd have been killed?' He pauses. 'You know, I've never thought about it that way. But now that you say it, yes, something like that could have happened.'

'Speaking of which, what finally happened to Master Wilson and his wife?'

'Well, we left them there, didn't we? Him hanging by his ankles from that tree, and his wife shackled to that pole.'

'What do you think is going to happen to them?'

'Somebody is going to find them. Another group of War Veterans. There are many of us moving around the country, taking over farms, and doing different things to them. I do not have the stomach for farming. This country is up for grabs, darling. Mugabe and his dogs are wolfing down the economy in big chunks. Those of us who served alongside him in the Bush War have to find other creative means of rewarding ourselves. A coup won't serve anyone's purpose. Killing Mugabe would only dig this country deeper into the quagmire.'

'So what is to be done?'

'You're sounding like a revolutionary, comrade sister. *What is to be done?*' He smiles. 'We'll just nibble at the corners of this big cake, and no one will even notice. The IMF and the UN and the World Bank won't even realise it. That's fair, isn't it? Those august bodies don't even know we exist. They'll point fingers at Mugabe. We're faceless, on the margins, my dear.'

She says, 'Okay, so what are you going to do with us?'

'As I was saying to you, this is a new game for me. This is my first mission of its kind, so to speak.'

'So, that's what it is, a game. We are just toys to you?'

'You're putting it crudely.'

'But it is the truth, isn't it?'

There's a softness to his voice, to his manner when he says, 'You don't understand.' She can sense some uncertainty, some doubt. Her head feels light.

He says, 'There might be some complications down the line.' He nods to himself. 'Yes, some complications.'

'What are you talking about?'

'You see, at some stage we're going to hand you over. Hand you over to the Congolese we are working with on this mission. There are some Congolese and South Africans involved. I don't know how that is going to pan out. There's also a likelihood that the group will be split in two: some will go to the Congo, others to South Africa. Either way, all of you will be issued South African identity documents before we leave this place.'

His tongue has been loosened by the brown-brown. Or was it the sex? Did he sense some honesty in that moment? Did he trust her more now? Either way, she has to concentrate. This is important. He is giving his secrets away. 'Why?' she asks.

'If we get stopped by United Nations peace monitors, and other nosy types, we can always show our documents – that we are proper labour recruiters, and you guys are recruits. In fact, I have an identity document that proves I am in the employ of New Africa Mining in the Congo, in charge of security. I protect their property. And you are their property.'

'Just like that?'

'Yes, just like that.'

'But you sound so uncertain.'

'I've never done this before, to be honest.'

Queenface sits up, legs tucked in beneath her. 'If you are so scared, why don't you turn us loose? It's not as if we are going to tell the police or anything. We don't know who you truly are, or where you come from. Just turn us loose and this will all be over.'

'Turn you loose and throw away money, and offend my partners who might kill me?'

She suppresses the urge to reassure him. *Him!* Her captor! She shakes her head, and tries to concentrate. She gathers that she and her neighbours are going to be sold, somehow, to some Congolese. Sold to do what in the Congo, she has yet to fathom. Which Congo anyway? Congo-Brazzaville or Congo-Kinshasa? She doesn't want to show her anxiety. She must play it cool.

He says, 'We're not human traffickers. Ever heard of human traffickers?'

'We might be farmworkers, but we're not exactly from Mars. We know what's happening in this world. We have relatives in England, Canada, South Africa. They write us letters. I am the professional letter writer and letter reader for our farm, seeing as I am the most educated.'

'As I was saying, we're not human traffickers. No. We work for an NGO. We are recruiting workers for some mines in the Congo and South Africa.'

She laughs sarcastically. 'They work for an NGO!' She throws her head back, still in paroxysms of mirth. 'You're the first NGO people who move around with big guns. The first NGOs who harass farmers and kidnap people.' She laughs again. 'And quite frankly, you're the first NGO that doesn't have a white face. NGO people are white people. Try another tack, brother.'

Major-General Chenjerai is clearly a man of power, control. Queenface doesn't quite know where she gets the nerve to contradict him in this manner. But he doesn't seem to mind. In fact, he looks amused. 'As I was saying to you,' he says, 'mine is to facilitate the recruitment. While everyone is going to the mines, you are staying with me! You are mine.' He takes her hand and kisses it.

'I've been meaning to ask you, Queenface: you are young, intelligent, attractive, but why haven't you left this hellhole of a country? Why did you subject yourself to Master Wilson's yoke? You could go to Botswana, South Africa, even England and get yourself a job. The truth shall set you free! And the truth can be arrived at via the corridor of a full disclosure.'

'After my parents were killed during the Gukurahundi,' she begins, 'I was adopted by distant relatives who had survived the genocide. We fled from the communal lands and they found refuge with Master Wilson. When my adopted parents were about to die, they made me promise I would not leave the farm, that I would remain loyal to Master Wilson. That's why I stayed.' She does not mention her sister or her nieces. She does not want him to know that she has family here, to draw attention to them. There's no telling how he would react. Would he jealously separate her from them to keep her all to himself? 'But apart from that, I did not really feel the compulsion to leave Matabeleland. I heard that my relatives lived a glamorised form of slavery in England and Canada. They cleaned white people's toilets, they lived in overcrowded conditions – and, most depressingly, the weather is said to be quite cruel. I felt I could live with the hell that I was used to. I was prepared to live on the farm day by day. I felt that was my fate.'

He shakes his head. 'When I was a child, and my father had to slaughter a sheep, he always felt highly agitated, muttering under his breath, "Stupid sheep, stupid sheep. I hate sheep." And I would ask, "But, Father, sheep gives good meat, unlike smelly goat." My father would burst out, "But sheep give up without a fight! A sheep doesn't bleat or roar. We believe an animal must make noise when we slaughter it, because the noise it makes connects us to the world yonder, the spiritual world. A sheep dies without a fight, without even a squeak." Now when I look at you, I see one who is as resigned as a sheep that's about to be slaughtered.'

'Not any more. You've woken me up from my slumber of stupidity. I don't care what you're going to do with us, I am prepared for the challenge now. The fighter in me has been revived.'

He smiles at her. 'So, I'm the bright ray of sunshine in your life that has come to save you from a dull existence?'

If she had the power, she would smack him. But she keeps mum. She does not correct his misinterpretation.

She looks at the Bible with the traces of brown-brown still visible on the cover. She remembers the Bible story of the woman who took a tent pen and drove it through her enemy's skull when he was asleep. Her eyes scan the walls of the tent.

'What are you looking at?' he asks.

'Nothing. Where are Mrs Wilson's clothes that you brought for me to wear?'

He points to a suitcase.

She takes a dress from the suitcase and puts it on. Then she works herself into a pair of Mrs Wilson's panties. She is not used to panties. Back at Golden Meadows she owns only three pairs which she wears on special occasions. During the week, like every woman on the farm, she walks around in a long dress or pinafore, with the wind cooling her essentials. Even on Saturday, going to church, she doesn't wear panties. They irritate her. They are restrictive, invasive.

But the soldier man insisted, as they were leaving Golden Meadows, that she take as many pairs from Mrs Wilson's closet as possible. 'You need to start behaving like a civilised lady, my darling. Where I'm taking you, they wear shoes and decent dresses. They wear colourful underwear and socks. Ladies walk around enveloped in perfume, not the smell of cow dung. Their hair is properly oiled and designed. Their lips shine with lip gloss. I'm taking you to the heart of civilisation.'

They leave the tent. The minute her feet touch the ground outside, she winces. As a rule, she only wears shoes when going to church or on those special occasions the Wilsons treat the workers to a drive to the city of Bulawayo. Now, in this furnace of a place, she finds she needs to wear shoes. She goes back to the tent to put on the sneakers she swiped from Mrs Wilson's bedroom.

This corner of the world where they have ended up is a wasteland of sun-scorched grass, stunted trees, sharp rocks jutting out of the ground. The sky is as pale as a dry bone. Her eyes hurt; everything seems extra bright. In the distance she can make out what used to be a house. The roof is gone. The windows are ghastly sockets in this skeleton of a house. As far as the eye can see, there is not much life – apart from two kites circling the sky. Every now and then a dust devil breaks into a frenzied dance. Only to die again. She smiles momentarily when her eyes behold a river further down to the right. A clump of willows along the banks.

'Hey, hey,' his voice is stern, 'where do you think you're going?'

She whirls around, says, 'I am going to the river. I need to wash.'

'Who gave you permission?'

She shrugs.

'We are going over there,' he says, pointing. His face is dark, threatening. No more Mr Nice Guy.

Her eyes follow his finger. 'A church! That's where the singing came from this morning! Wow. Where are we?'

The church is a few hundred metres from where she is standing. It's a simple structure made of stones. They start walking briskly towards it. As they approach, she notices that the church's door looks out of place. It's a modern door made of strong wood, with intricate designs. She looks up at the steeple. There's a cross at the top of it.

She repeats, 'Where are we?'

'Not for you to know.' His voice is stern, unlike the soft baritone that was singing praises to her beauty not so long ago. 'Come, let's join the others inside the church.' The singing has resumed.

There are soldiers patrolling the yards. Some of her fellow farmworkers, the women, are tending cooking fires under a tree. They look up from their pots and fires as she and the soldier walk past. There is malevolence in their eyes. Queenface looks for her sister, but does not see her. Magwegwe is sitting on an upturned drum not far from the cooking women. He is playing his guitar, humming a melancholy song. He does not look up when Queenface calls out his name in greeting. Two teardrops plop onto the strings of his guitar.

Queenface and Major-General Chenjerai enter the church. It takes her a few moments before her eyes adjust to the darkness inside. Then familiar faces beam at her. The women and children are singing animatedly, clapping hands. There is Perseverance, with Nomfundo and Nozizwe, taking part with enthusiasm. The men are just droning along, their hearts clearly not in the singing at all.

Queenface looks long and hard at the pulpit. An emaciated

Christ on the cross stares back at her. He's the blackest Christ she's ever seen. His hair shoulder-length black curls.

'Okay, lovely people,' one of the soldiers says, after the singing has faded out, 'now we're going to have breakfast. Do you people want food?'

'Yeeeees!' scream the children.

'Okay, before we go out for breakfast, you will listen carefully to me. We are going to do exactly what we did last night. What we call roll call. We want to be sure everyone is still here, that no one has been stolen by hyenas. You need to be accounted for, because today we are going to give you documents that will be your key to a bright future. In order to go to that bright future, we need to capture you, your name, your age and everything. Now we are going to do roll call.'

Magwegwe walks in just in time for roll call. Major-General Chenjerai disappears outside for a while. Queenface finally moves to Perseverance, Nomfundo and Nozizwe, and gives them each a quick hug. 'We need to get away,' she says to Perseverance, as soon as possible, 'otherwise we will be sold. I will get away from the major-general and come find you. Then we must run.' Chenjerai re-enters the church and Queenface quickly moves away from her family. The major-general is now accompanied by a man in an ill-fitting cream cassock and black dog collar.

A friendly smile on his face, the priest intones, 'Permit the children to come to Me; do not hinder them; for the Kingdom of God belongs to such as these. Verily, verily, I say unto you, whoever does not receive the Kingdom of God like a child will not enter it at all.'

Reluctantly at first, children start gravitating towards him.

In turn, each is rewarded with a sweet. The man of God gets them singing a common church song.

The children are jiving to the song, delivered in fast-tempo, staccato style – 'We are marching over to Jerusalem, we're marching over to Jerusalem. Jeh-ru-sah-lem, Jerusalema-ha-ha. Marching over to Jerusalem, Jeh-ru-sah-lem . . . Jerusalema-ha-ha!'

When they hit the staccato part they quiver like reeds agitated by a strong gust of wind.

The people file out of the church in two orderly lines: women and children form one line, and men have their own. The lines snake all the way to the furthest corner of the compound where women are busy with huge pots.

Breakfast is thick porridge and left-over meat from yesterday. Amahewu, a sludgy drink made from fermented maize porridge, is frothing from an enormous drum. After the rich breakfast, each camp inmate is given a big mug of the amahewu to wash down the food. Suddenly everyone wants to go and sleep, so thick and heavy was the breakfast.

Queenface needs to relieve herself. She is not feeling too well. The powder she took earlier on is making her sweat.

'May I go to the toilet, please,' she asks Major-General.

'We don't have a proper toilet, you know. Anyway, you're used to squatting behind bushes. Ask one of the soldiers to walk you down to the river where you can do your business.' He pauses. 'Better still, let me walk you.'

When they get to the river, Queenface asks the major-general, 'Will you give me some privacy?'

He laughs. 'I need to keep an eye on you.'

She takes off her panties and squats. She looks away from

him, to the river. There are some dead fish floating in the water. A cloud of flies congregates around it.

A loud bang sounds out. More bangs. Gunfire!

Queenface jumps up, pulls up her panties. The major-general grabs her arm. His eyes are wild. 'Come!'

They run towards the shots. Now there is silence. The major-general runs ahead. He is very fast. She could run the opposite way, but he would easily be able to catch her. And she has to know: who was shot? Not Perseverance, not Nomfundo, not Nozizwe. Oh, please, no.

They see soldiers ahead of them.

'What the hell are they doing?' shouts Major-General Chenjerai. He runs towards the men. She follows.

A bloodied corpse lies at their feet.

'And what is this!' says Major-General. 'What happened?'

The soldiers snap to attention. 'Major-General, sir, he was trying to run away, to escape.'

'And you killed him? You're fucking with my money, captain, you're fucking with my money. Do you know how much one of them is worth? And where do you think your salary is going to come from, if you kill the goose that lays the golden egg? Soldier, soldier! Use your fucking brain! Did you have to kill him? Why didn't you chase him until you caught him?'

'He was far ahead. We noticed it too late. We couldn't take the risk of letting him go. So I ordered the comrades to shoot to kill.'

It is a man, Queenface realises with relief. Then she looks at the corpse again. Oh, shit! It is Magwegwe! Oh fuck, Magwegwe. Queenface is sobbing now. A soldier leads her away from the corpse. Poor Magwegwe – he had loved her. She suddenly feels guilty. She thinks being seen in the company of the senior soldier might have made Magwegwe lose hope, lose interest in her.

More soldiers and some farmworkers arrive. Major-General addresses the farmworkers: 'You see, you assholes, you are making my soldiers spill blood unnecessarily! It is not our mission to kill, but you are forcing our hand. Go and tell your wives over there in that church, tell your children, tell your neighbours that whoever tries to run away shall be killed. We shoot to kill, motherfuckers. You don't fuck with us!'

He unholsters his gun, points it at one of the farmworkers. 'Are you going to try to run?'

'No, sir, I won't.'

'You are lying to me. Given a chance, any sane man would run for it. Every single one of you is dreaming up an escape plan. I know that! Now, listen carefully.' He takes two steps, places the barrel of the gun on the man's temple. 'If I see you attempting an escape, I will chase you until I catch you. None of you can outrun me. Ask my soldiers. I can run. Then after catching you, I'll bring you back to camp. I'll strip you naked in front of your women, your children. What will I do?'

The man, sobbing now, says, 'You will strip me naked . . .'

'And then what will I do next? Answer me, dammit, what will I do?'

'I . . . I don't know . . .'

'Use your imagination! What would you do to a naked enemy, in front of women and children? In my position, what would you do?'

'I would shoot you . . . in . . . front . . . of the . . . children . . . the women . . .'

'Is your wife among those women?'

'Yes, sir.'

'Any children?'

'Yes, three.'

'So, you know what I'm going to do to you in front of your wife and three children.'

'You'll shoot me in front of them.'

'There is no imagination there. I will not shoot you. I'll get my hunting knife, cut off your dick first. What will I do?'

'Cut off my dick first.'

'Then I'll cut your balls off. Then I'll push them into your mouth! And you will chew them, eat them! In front of your wife and three children. That's what I'll do. I swear to God. If any of your friends is thinking of an escape, approaches you with a plan to escape, do not hesitate to come to me. Come and tell me. Do you hear me?'

'Yes, sir.'

He spits into the unlucky man's face.

Queenface is shaking and sweating. She bends over and throws up. When she straightens, she feels as if some of the horror and fear has been purged from her. She has seen that the major-general is a fast runner, but she thinks she's got the soldier's weakness all figured out. She must strike while she still has the chance. Anxious and apprehensive though she is, she'll just have to wait until nightfall. When night finally falls, and she gets to pounce on her prey, she will have to do so with precision and ferocity. For there will be no second chances.

Ancestral Voices

When Fikile left the United States two weeks ago, her native city of Boston was shivering under a thick white blanket of snow. Which is why, in the two weeks she's been in South Africa, sweating and gasping for breath under sunny skies, she's had to pause every now and then to look around her, and think: *Am I dreaming or what?*

A native of North America will always associate Christmastime with people groaning under layers of clothing as they grudgingly trudge along snow-covered pavements.

Now she is in her bathing suit, lazing around on a chaise longue, under a beach umbrella, next to her auntie Promise's pool in Houghton.

Fikile spies her auntie Promise walking hurriedly towards her. Face highly made up, and her slim body dressed in a low-cut top, jeans and high heels, it is clear Auntie Promise is not coming towards the swimming pool for a quick dip in the water. There's evidently something important on her mind. 'Girl, you need to get dressed. We need to go!'

Fikile pushes her sunglasses down onto her nose and peers over them. 'Go where, Auntie?'

'Ah . . . it's a surprise. You'll see.'

Her auntie has planned another fun South African outing

for her – how exciting! Would they go to a park or a mall or go see wild animals at a game reserve? She searches Auntie Promise's face for clues, but only sees agitation. Wow, she must really want to get out of the house.

'Okay, Auntie, I'll go change.'

They arrive in Soweto half an hour later. The Soweto that presses its face against the windows of her aunt's car now is different from the glamorous Vilakazi Street she was taken to just a few days after her arrival in South Africa. In that famous street in Orlando West, where Nelson Mandela and Archbishop Desmond Tutu's houses have been turned into museums, rowdy restaurants teemed with tourists. 'This Vilakazi of ours is the only street in the world that boasts two Nobel laureates,' their tour guide had said.

The part of Soweto they are driving through this afternoon looks . . . Menacing is the right word. At the appearance of the car, children take a break from kicking a makeshift soccer ball, put together with bunched-up plastic bags and string. They close in on the silver BMW – some coming from the front, others approaching from the sides. Auntie Promise has to slow down or risk running them down. Fikile is not comfortable looking them straight in the eye. There is no awe or deference in their eyes. Not even anger or insolence. Only an eerie hollowness. Fikile wants to suggest that her aunt throw some banknotes at them, as is her wont. But then she realises that rolling down the window would not be an advisable thing to do.

They turn to the right, then to the left. This street vomits them into a dirt road. Modest houses line the dirt road, exactly the same as the hundreds of others they've just seen – four-roomed matchbox houses with asbestos roofs squatting behind rusty fences. No children here. Two dogs cantering down the street. Pausing every now and then to investigate a mound of trash. An old man trudging home. Tired or drunk, judging by his erratic, half-hearted progress. Two middle-aged women. One pushing a wheelbarrow, the other one eating corn. A plastic bucket is balanced expertly on top of the corn-eating woman's head. Her hips swaying ever so slightly.

'Here we are, then,' Auntie Promise says. No cheerfulness in her voice. They've stopped in front of what, to Fikile's eyes, looks like a burnt-out shell of a house. It stands behind a rusty, sagging fence. The two houses flanking it also seem abandoned. But they are in much better shape. There, the windows are still intact, albeit with no curtains, and the yards show only vague signs of neglect.

But at the house that is seemingly their destination the window frames are gaping holes. The sagging asbestos roof is a darkened grey. Armies of shrubs and weeds have taken over the yard. They are now waging war against each other, the dandelions appearing to conquer their various adversaries. Fikile expects ancient tombstones to sprout in between the tall weeds. Zombies to emerge therefrom. Not unlike Michael Jackson's 'Thriller' video.

'You mean here?' Fikile jerks a thumb at the house, just to be sure.

'Will you get out of the car!'

The two women they passed a few moments ago are now just across the street from the house. They look at Fikile and her aunt. The older woman utters something to her friend. Her wheelbarrow shrieks as she picks up speed. Her friend throws away her half-finished corn. The bucket, sitting on the crown of her head, wobbles precariously, almost toppling forward. Her right hand shoots up to steady it back into position.

'Did you hear what those crones said?' Auntie Promise is smiling sardonically.

'They muttered something in a language I cannot follow . . .'

'Sotho speakers. They called me the daughter of a ghost and a wizard.'

'Why?'

Auntie Promise shrugs, giggles. She leads the way through the rickety gate. An angry fire must have been let loose on this house years ago, Fikile thinks as she studies the blackened walls of the house.

'Why are we here, Auntie? This house looks abandoned. It looks haunted, even.'

Just then, she is shaken by a sharp cry coming from some-where beyond the bushes. 'What's that?'

Then she spots it: a lone goat tethered to a tree. She gasps.

Peaches are hanging yellow and plump from the tree. Some have fallen to the ground, forming a carpet that buzzes with insects. A basin of water and a bale of grass are laid out in front of the goat. When it sees them, the goat tries to run away, straining at the tether, the rope eating into its throat with each attempt. There is foam around its mouth. It bleats again, a low mournful sound. Fikile, her voice reduced to a whisper, says, 'Auntie, whose place is this?'

'Will you shut up and do as I do?'

A cart drawn by two donkeys comes rolling down the street. The man sitting in the cart is shouting, advertising his wares – maize, cabbages. When the cart comes alongside the house, the man's eyes grow big in what seems like sudden recognition.

He whips his donkeys with ferocity. The animals break into a fast canter.

Auntie Promise smiles at the fleeing vegetable merchant, reaches out her hand. The door to the house opens with a loud creak. They are in what looks like a kitchen now. A table in one corner. On the table, a two-plate burner. Next to the table, a lone chair. The other corner: an old-fashioned grocery cupboard, next to which is a sink. Then a small, old-fashioned fridge shuddering and humming softly. If there was a fire, not everything was burnt – or, more likely, Fikile reasons, the appliances were brought in after. When Auntie Promise opens the fridge, Fikile catches a glimpse of a modest collection of vegetables, a two-litre Coke, milk . . . Then her auntie shuts it again. From somewhere near the fridge, she reaches for a light switch. Bright light banishes the shadows that had been crowding around the room. Old, scuffed plastic tiles in a bilious green cover the floor. Some improvements clearly must have been made after the fire, but why not replace the windows, scrub the soot off the walls, repair the roof? What was this house being used for? Fikile wonders.

From the kitchen, they proceed to other rooms. The bedrooms smell of mildew and mothballs. Finally, they are in what appears to be a lounge. In this room, an old-fashioned television set sits on a sturdy coffee table. There's a two-seater sofa from which you can comfortably watch the television. Behind the sofa, an empty window. From all she's heard of crime in South Africa, Fikile is amazed that nobody has attempted to steal the TV through the open window frame. And passers-by seem to be avoiding the house – why? Auntie Promise opens a door leading to the backyard. Out here, there's a huge rockery which, in times gone by, would have been elegant, suffused with colour. Now it is overgrown with weeds. But sticking out of the profusion of weeds, unperturbed by it, is a beautiful rosebush in full bloom.

When she lifts her eyes, Fikile sees a white dove sitting on the top branch of a tree that stands at the extreme corner of the yard. It has to be the biggest dove Fikile has ever seen. It's the size of a small chicken. Almost. It's completely white, with luminous red eyes.

When it sees them, the dove seems to sigh, to relax, as if it'd been expecting them. Then the dove disappears. No, it does not fly away, or drop to the ground, or hide behind a branch. It simply disappears. Now it's here; now it's gone. Fikile blinks unbelievingly, frowns. Her aunt smiles.

With Auntie Promise leading the way, they wade through tall grass, around the house, until they are standing in front of the goat. The poor thing is now lying on the ground. At their approach, it lifts its head, gives them a look. No fear or excitement in its eyes. Resignation is all Fikile can read. Of course this is conjecture on her part, as she has no past experience with goats. She can't say that she understands goat behaviour. Once the goat has had a good look at them, it rests its head on the ground again and closes its eyes.

'Fikile, go and fetch the cooler box from the car,' Auntie Promise breaks into her thoughts. 'It's in the boot. Or the trunk, as you Americans would have it.'

She accepts the car keys from her aunt and starts picking her way through the tall grass.

Only when they sit down on two upturned beer crates, eating biltong and drinking Coke, does Auntie Promise start to answer

Fikile's questions. She says, 'You've been pestering me since we got here, Fikile, wanting to know what the hell we're doing here, what this spooky place is all about? "Spooky." What a word to use under the circumstances.'

Fikile nods, her mouth full of biltong.

'We've come here to listen to ancestral voices. Some Africans go to the graveyard to speak to their ancestors. Others trek away from the city, out to the bundu, the rural areas where they climb mountains, or wade deep into rivers to communicate with their ancestors. Sadly, we – you and I here – have none of those privileges. Our ancestral home is right here.' She points at the burnt-out house. 'This was your grandfather and grandmother's house. So, close your eyes, open your imagination, and think of this as my father's – your grandfather's – village. Think of this burnt-out shell as your grandpa's holy shrine.'

This is a different Auntie Promise from the person Fikile has got used to. The Auntie Promise of Houghton is loud and haughty, and in love with her fake American accent. This incarnation is soft-spoken, her delivery ponderous, deliberate.

This is the story Auntie Promise proceeds to tell her:

It was 1986. The country was on the boil. The apartheid government was living on borrowed time. They knew this. That is why they started unleashing their police force on the oppressed masses. Vicious kicks of a dying horse. Soldiers and covert killing squads were running amok. The black community was divided right down the middle as a result. There was one side that believed the government was serious about introducing reforms that would put all South Africans – black, white, Indian, coloured – on an equal footing when it came to jobs, education, health care and other amenities.

Then on the other side: a revolutionary school which held that apartheid could not be reformed. It had to be fought, defeated and buried. But the time for debate was long gone. The two sides were speaking to each other through petrol bombs. Through pangas. Through spears and clubs. Through guns. The government used the state of confusion and lawlessness to its advantage – arming one side against the other. Distrust and back-stabbing became the order of the day. Brother killed brother. Father sacrificed son at the altar of political expedience. If members of the same family, 'children from the same scrotum', as the Zulu saying goes, killed each other over political allegiances, imagine what mere neighbours, erstwhile friends did to one another!

By the time the political violence started, Fikile's own father had long left the country. He would later write regular letters to his family, to tell them he had finished his studies in the US. He would inform them that he had met and married an American woman. Some in the family were happy at the news, others shocked, angered and disappointed at their son's decision to take an American for a wife – not just any American, but a white one! But they'd been thrilled to see a picture of 'their' daughter Fikile, born at the start of the new millennium, the year 2000. Although yellow in complexion, she bore the famous facial features that the Gumedes esteemed highly: thick proud lips, chubby cheeks, sharp-pointed ears that reminded one of a character in *Star Trek* and a nose to match. The Gumedes were also comforted by the fact that their son had given his mixed-race daughter a Zulu name – Fikile. *She Has Arrived*. He'd given her this name after his new wife had endured a number of miscarriages. To thank God and the ancestors for his first-born. His wife was amused by the meaning and rationale behind the name. But it made a lot of sense to her; it was also memorable and unique in a country where black girls were called La Toya or La Shonda or La Dashia.

So, when the violence broke out in 1986, Fikile's grandparents, Philomena and Caiphus Gumede, were living all by themselves in the township.

Their first-born son was studying in America, their daughter, their second-born, in prison for political reasons. A third son was dead. Their baby daughter, Promise, was in boarding school in Durban.

Old Gumede and his wife were now by themselves in the house, lonely and dejected. Those who'd known the Gumedes as a politically committed family were either in prison, or in exile, or dead. A new generation had come up to fill the vacuum. A generation that couldn't give a fuck about who Caiphus Gumede was. All these kids saw was an old man whose yard was becoming a forest – with all these trees and herbs.

The anti-apartheid liberation movement in exile said: make the country ungovernable, so that you bring the government to its knees.

Suddenly there was a new brand of activist on the street. The activist who shoots. Burns. Stabs. Clobbers. And asks questions later. He was called the Comrade.

The Comrade carried a box of matches and a car tyre. When circumstances demanded, he would douse the tyre in petrol, hang it around the neck of a suspected apartheid collaborator, before setting it alight. Burn the collaborator. Burn the witch.

'But how do we identify these witchdoctors?' some eager, but cautious activists wanted to know.

It was said the witches were the ones who did not attend the activists' meetings. They were the ones who sent their children to boarding schools out of town.

The witches were supposedly the ones who asked too many questions. You don't ask questions in the middle of a revolution. Questions breed doubt. Doubt is fertile ground for defeat.

They said the witches were the old men and women who skulked behind their fences, looking at the activists through slightly parted curtains as they fought pitched battles against the police and the army.

Even if your only crime was not cleaning your yard, you were thought to be a witch. They would ask why you had a profusion of trees in your yard – what were you hiding there.

'Let us go and get the witches!' they said.

Embers of ancient resentments and animosities were retrieved from the corners where they had been smouldering. Winds of distrust blew fiercely. To rekindle and fan the embers until they glowed and burned with a purposeful intensity. Some older members of the community whispered names into the ears of their grandchildren, the Comrades: 'Mr So-and-so is a wizard! He rides a baboon at night! He concocts medicine that is neutralising your efforts at liberating this country.'

The Comrades nodded their understanding. They didn't need much cajoling and convincing. Their fingers were always itchy for action. So they obliged their grandparents, uncles and aunts. The witches were dragged out of their houses. Stripped naked. Paraded up and down the streets. Forced to make public confessions:

'I am a witch, I am a witch. It is I who gave the police magical muthi that helped them locate and unearth the arms cache that the Comrades had buried over there.'

One night, Caiphus Gumede and his wife were in bed in their home.

Then:

Excited voices in the street. Dogs barking. Men whistling. Women ululating. On the tarred surface of the road, feet thudding. Somebody beating a tin drum – *gong-gong-gong*!

Caiphus sat up in bed. He said, 'KaMkhabela, get dressed! Quick! Out of bed.'

'But why?' his Philomena asked, wiping her eyes.

'We have to go and join those kids in the street.'

'But why?'

'We have to be seen to be part of their movement'

'But we are not; we are not killers.'

Then: a loud crash. Somebody had lobbed a brick through the window.

Agitated movement on the premises.

A voice: 'This is the biggest wizard around! Gumede!'

And another: 'He keeps baboons and tokoloshes in his bedroom.'

'The sell-out!'

'He can't be allowed to leave the house!'

Stones and other missiles started raining on the roof of the house. *Click-clack. Click-clack. Clack-clack!*

A ball of fire flew through the bedroom window and landed on the bed. A Molotov cocktail. *Pfooo-bam!*

It was soon followed by another one. *Pfoooo!*

And yet another one. *Pfooo-pfooo-bam!*

Walls of fire were closing in on the Gumedes trapped in their own bedroom.

'Bulalan'abathakathi! Kill the witches!'

Gumede shouted: 'But, Comrades, we are all comrades. My children died for this struggle. My children are in jail for this struggle. My children are in exile for this struggle. You should have asked your grandparents and your parents about me.'

It was hard to hear him above the thunderous roar of the flames. No one cared anyway.

Gumede was coughing, choking on the smoke. His wife enveloped him in a tight, passionate hug, but never uttered a cry. Stuck in a corner, they began twitching and jumping involuntarily as the heat intensified. Even the tiled floor on which they stood was a furnace.

There was singing and shouting outside.

Fiery fangs of yellow flames bit into the old couple's entwined bodies. Bodies seeking comfort and strength in each other. Bodies drenched in sweat. Philomena's old, flimsy terylene nightdress began to shrink and melt. The molten plastic dripped down her legs, clung to her skin. Jaws clenched, muscles tensed, eyes shut, she did not cry as the burning plastic stung her bare skin. She never let go of her husband. His pyjamas caught fire. Butterflies of fire were fluttering about his body. Yet the two of them never let go of each other. They coughed and vomited.

They could have cried. They could have hollered. They could have begged: *We're sorry! Please, we are sorry. Somebody help! Have mercy on poor old people! Help!*

But they never cried out. Not to beg for mercy. Not to acknowledge the searing agony of fire on exposed skin. They wouldn't give the searing flames the pleasure. Instead, it was the flames that cried out. The flames cried out in frustration at those old people who wouldn't admit defeat, who wouldn't beg for mercy.

They were still outside the Gumede house, the marauders. Somebody fired a gun into the air. A woman ululated.

Still in each other's arms, and to the tumultuous music of the flames, Gumede and his wife started moving about the room in a macabre waltz of death. Their skin was sizzling like pieces of bacon in a skillet.

It was a long time before the Gumedes finally collapsed to the floor. Exhausted. There were occasional triumphant noises – *pfoof-pfoof-pfoof!* – as the fire ate with relish and satisfaction into their hair, flesh, cartilage. Hours later, the flames succumbed to their own mortality. They were humble, harmless cinders glowing weakly then. The attackers were gone. The night resumed its indifferent, dignified silence. Not even dogs dared to bark.

Fikile is sobbing freely now, her shoulders jerking uncontrollably. Her quiet sobs come from a deep dark corner which, until then, she never realised she possessed. Her aunt lets her be.

While her aunt had been talking, Fikile could hear it. The music of violence. The murmuring, complaining, wailing, shouting, screaming, hollering, raging, roaring flames. A cyclone of violence that consumes everything around it. In front of it. Consumes itself even.

The whole experience is, for Fikile, vertiginous. She is falling down the abyss of history. She is being swallowed by history. Claimed by it. Then vomited out again by it.

Fikile's skin is singing with pain from the furious flames of South African history. She might have a South African-sounding name – Fikile Gumede-Salter, but she's as American as apple pie and beef jerky. She loves the United States, would die for her country. Stories of 9/11 always drive her to tears, even though she was but a baby when the Twin Towers fell. She's never thought she'd feel the same about any other country. For, let's face it, South Africa was not her country. It was her father's country. And her father has been dead for a year now. Though she'd never met her grandparents, her father's power of evocation when he used to speak about his country, combined with her own powerful imagination, never failed to bring them to life. But she hadn't imagined she would be this moved by them, by their story.

The sky darkens. The breeze that's been wafting about gathers strength. Soon it's making tumultuous music through tree branches. The trees shudder.

Fikile lifts her head, wipes her eyes, shivers. Goose pimples break out on her arms. The dove she saw earlier has returned. It sits, unmoving, on the branch of the tree above her. Fikile is looking at it, her heart thumping. The dove looks to the left. A second dove appears next to it. Just like a rabbit appearing at the tip of a magician's wand. The second bird is as big as the other. The birds look each other in the eye. Then they focus their attention on Fikile. The doves start cooing. It's a forlorn song that drifts into the atmosphere. Somewhere in the distance, a dog breaks into a series of staccato barks, offering a bizarre syncopation to the music of the doves. Fikile closes her eyes to listen and make sense of the music. Perhaps it is her imagination going wild. When she opens her eyes, the doves are still there. She closes her eyes, then opens them quickly. The doves are gone. But the melodious echo of their voices remains.

Fikile looks at her aunt in amazement. Then a new sound rents the air, a noise that sounds like the beating of a great many bird wings. Now the yard is white as snow. Doves everywhere. Some young, some old. Some small, some as big as the first two doves. There is agitation in their voices as they coo. The sky opens to release a slight drizzle. Then: thin, silvery spikes of rain. Soon the raindrops become as fat as overfed spiders. They plop on the exposed arms of Fikile and her aunt. Thunder rumbles. Strobes of lightning momentarily turn the sky into a cracked car windscreen. God coughs from His heavens.

'Let's go inside, Fikzo. I have to finish this story. I won't be telling it in instalments. It's not a TV serial. It has to be told today, in its entirety.'

They duck inside the house. The asbestos roof leaks in places. They find a corner in the lounge where the water does not reach them. They sit on empty beer crates they've brought from outside.

Auntie Promise picks up the threads:

'Now the day of the funeral. Members of the Gumede family, from far and near, had been alerted. They went to the local mortuary. The idea was to collect the scorched remains of your grandfather and grandmother. It was only a day before my parents' funeral that I got to hear about the horrific deaths, in the first place. Remember, there were no cellphones then. No one had been able to reach me, tell me what happened. It didn't help that the country was in a State of Emergency. Newspapers got told what to report, and how to report it. Only the day before the funeral did I get to hear about what happened. I rushed home.

'Under police escort some relatives – uncles and aunts whom

I'd met when I was still very young – were with me at the mortuary. The women were asked to stand in the reception area while the men ventured deep into the section where they keep the corpses. About thirty minutes later, the men came back. Much as they tried to put on brave faces, you could see they'd been crying. The police helped to load the two coffins into police vans – no hearses! That's when I started crying. The remains of my parents were being carted off in police vans. Even in death, they were still being humiliated! When we reached the house . . .' She looks at Fikile as if she had asked a question. 'Yes, can you believe that the police said if we wanted to have a proper vigil at the local hall, we'd have to accept that they'd be there, watching us. If, however, we wanted to hold a private vigil, we had to go and conduct it at our house. Yes, at the remains of this very house. The house was still cloaked in a strong stench of death, and the smell of fire. But we chose to have our vigil here, with a measure of dignity, rather than having the police walking up and down the aisles in the public hall. It turned out to be the longest night of my life. One of the elders had expressly told everyone that the bodies of our parents were not to be viewed under any circumstances. I fought a losing battle.

'Early the following day, people from our neighbourhood – the very people who had long abandoned their houses – poured onto our yard, singing revolutionary songs. I could imagine some of those songs were sung as my parents were being attacked. But every revolution has its unintended casualty, I have been told. There are others, the older set, who were singing church songs. Songs meant to console us. Hearses from the mortuary rocked up. It was all very confusing. The previous night, the police had refused us permission to transport the coffins in hearses, but that day two police vans were there, escorting two hearses. As soon as the police arrived, many of the mourners snuck out of our yard. They disappeared into thin air. Again, the neighbourhood was like a wasteland. No life whatsoever in the streets.

'A man from another section of the township, a lay preacher who once worked with my father at one of the factories, had volunteered to conduct the service. It was brave of him. Many local priests had refused to preside over funeral services of "revolutionary types". No one wanted to find themselves on the wrong side of the government.

'So the cortege of nine cars, one minibus taxi, and two police vans snaked along the road, towards Avalon Cemetery. The cemetery was a hive of activity. There were so many police and army vehicles at the graveyard, it was as if we'd come to a military parade—'

An explosive sound erupts outside. Auntie Promise and Fikile sit up, startled. The sound grows in volume. Now it's clear: it is the thunderous thud of African drums. It inspires the goat to start bleating most horrendously.

Auntie Promise smiles. 'They have come. They are here.'

'Who is it, Auntie? Shouldn't we go and see what's happening?'

'You sit down – they'll come to us.'

'Who?'

Then there is a voice raised in what sounds to Fikile like the praise poetry her father made her listen to a long time ago.

The voice comes closer and closer to where they are sitting.

Fikile recognises the language as Zulu, but she knows too little to understand what is being said.

Finally, the speaker of the words shows his face at the door, followed by a group of men and women bearing loads of pumpkins, carrots, cabbages and other gifts. Raindrops shine in their hair and on the produce in their hands.

Without even taking a second glance at Auntie Promise and Fikile, the procession moves into the tiny lounge area and the people deposit their gifts in a corner.

When the poet has stopped his recitation, and the music has died, one of the men bows before Auntie Promise, smiling.

'What took you so long, Bernard?' says Auntie Promise in an even voice, speaking in English.

'Sorry, sister, there's been a shortage of taxis since they started fighting again.'

Then they revert to Zulu, and Fikile is lost. At length, Auntie Promise says in English, 'We don't have much time to waste, Bernard. The sun has long fallen. The ceremony must begin before it's too late.'

'Always efficient, Big Sister. Eyes always on the ball. We shall get started.' For the first time, Bernard focuses his eyes on Fikile. He says in English, 'I believe this is the little girl from overseas?'

'The one and only,' says Auntie Promise.

Bernard clears his throat, mouths words silently, before he spits them out all at the same time in an accent he probably thinks is American: 'Hello-how-are-you-welcome-home.' Then he smiles, and looks at Fikile expectantly. The other women and men in the room hold their collective breath, clearly waiting to hear what the girl from overseas is going to say.

Fikile says, 'I'm good, thank you very much, sir. And thank you for . . . thank you for the warm welcome.'

The entire room sighs. There are whispers:

'You heard that?'

'Couldn't make out what she said.'

'True American English is hard to grasp.'

'Speaking through her nostrils, you heard.'

'And she's one of us – she's a Gumede.'

Bernard says, 'Thank-you-welcome-home-young-sister-Fikile.' Then he pauses, gathering his thoughts, and proceeds in Zulu, addressing Auntie Promise.

Auntie Promise turns to Fikile. 'He is saying the ceremony is about to begin.'

'What is this ceremony you keep talking about?'

'To introduce you to the ancestors. We will now slaughter the goat.'

'What the hell! You can't be serious.' Fikile looks at her aunt in horror.

Auntie Promise has no time for her. She's busy jabbering away, barking out instructions left, right and centre.

It is raining harder outside. Water streams through the roof in some places. But those in the room seem unperturbed, their eyes focused on Fikile.

They bring the goat in. It's bleating furiously, trying to dig its hooves in the ground, gaining no traction. When they finally put it at the centre of the room, Auntie Promise says, 'Okay, Fikzo, come and kneel next to the goat.'

'No ways!'

Auntie Promise looks at Bernard, nods. Shrugging, and smiling at Fikile, Bernard grabs her around her waist, and drags her towards the goat. Fikile can't believe what's happening. 'No, no, *no!*' She claws his arms, trying to get loose. Two more men help pin her down, next to the goat. She screams and squirms in impotent rage.

Then she looks at the goat and sees her screams are upsetting it further. She holds her tongue but glares at the men pushing her down, making her lie next to the goat. She wriggles this way and that, trying to free herself from their grip, but to no avail. When she tries to bite their hands, her teeth snap at air.

Bernard speaks in Zulu, with Auntie Promise translating: 'Young lady, this is your goat. Do not be afraid of it. When we spill its blood, it will fight. It will bleat. That is the noise we want it to make so Izithutha – or The Stupid Ones, as we refer to our ancestors – will wake up and watch and listen to what we have to say on your behalf. We call them The Stupid Ones because in their eternal wisdom they know exactly who you are, and what you require of them, but you still have to be introduced to them. Which is why we are here. We have to ask them to protect you, to guide you. They need to be perpetually reminded of their responsibility to their progeny. The Stupid Ones. We also call them The Stupid Ones because if we stray from tradition handed from generation to generation, they descend on us with a vicious fury that one should reserve for one's worst enemies. Because of the wrath of The Stupid Ones, you can lose your loved one inexplicably. You can go mad. You can lose your job. Any calamity can befall you when you offend The Stupid Ones. The Stupid Ones know of you, yet they won't know you until they have been officially alerted to your puny existence through the spilling of blood, and the chanting of the proper clan praise names and the singing of the appropriate songs. The Stupid Ones.'

Someone brings an enamel plate heaped with a strange dry herb. Bernard lights the mound of herb. It burns with a soft, crackling sound. Tendrils of smoke rise to the air. He brings the plate next to the goat's nose. The animal starts sneezing. The aromatic smoke enters Fikile's nostrils. She sneezes uncontrollably.

Bernard continues and Auntie Promise interprets: 'This is called impepho, a sacred herb for occasions such as this. Yes, once provoked, the wrath of The Stupid Ones knows no bounds. They are all-seeing. I know you were born across the seas, but their fingers and hands of fury can reach across the tallest mountains, the biggest oceans. They can pry you from under the deepest bunker. And deal with you viciously. The Stupid Ones. They have all these powers because they sit at the feet of Mvelinqangi – The One Who Appeared First. Or, in the Christian Bible, the entity we call God. God sees all and knows all. God has sprinkled some sparks of His wisdom on the heads of The Stupid Ones. That is why The Stupid Ones can also see and know a lot. But they need to be reminded of their responsibility. I bet the reason we pray to God is because we also want to remind Him of His responsibility to us. He has too much on His plate.'

Bernard takes a long pause. Then he gently pushes Fikile's face against the hairy side of the goat, speaking softly: 'Here is your goat. Do not be afraid of it.'

Fikile does not need to be encouraged to rub her face against the side of the goat. It feels good to do so. The smoke of that herb is lulling her.

'Here is your goat. Do not be afraid of it . . .'

The first and last time Fikile saw a live goat was during a visit to a tourist farm in Cape Cod many years ago. But the goat she saw then had looked clean, as if straight out of a magazine or TV commercial. The coat looked as if it had been bleached, and painstakingly groomed, the horns and hooves polished. The goat sitting next to her now emits a pong that is intoxicating in its repugnance. She does her best to ignore the smell. She just lies next to the goat, sneezing continuously. For a moment she pauses to think what her friends back in Boston would make of this scene: the sharp-tongued Fikile 'Zulu Warrior' Gumede lying next to a goat and sneezing non-stop like that ugly witch in the *Shaka Zulu* TV series. She smiles to herself. Then she starts to giggle when she notices the goat has shat. The fresh pungent pellets look cute though, she has to admit. You could mistake them for exclusive candy-coated nuts from Hershey's. That shimmering green colour.

Fikile's eyes meet those of the goat. Ever so briefly. She can't help thinking that, were they meeting under different circumstances, they would have been friends. Fikile and the goat. She would have given the goat some succulent greens. Or some peanuts, even some ice cream. Yes, goats are herbivorous, but you can teach your pet to eat almost anything. Her father once told her of a goat from somewhere in Durban. A goat that ate meat, rice and drank beer, and – yes! – even smoked cigarettes. Dennis the Goat. That was the name of the goat. She had enjoyed the story of Dennis the Goat. Now she is looking at the nameless goat lying next to her. Had they met under different circumstances, she surely would have petted the goat, told it stories about . . . about America. But meeting under these compromised circumstances, she is somewhat angry, embarrassed that she can't even pet the goat – let alone save it from what is coming. Auntie Promise said they were going to kill the goat. Poor, poor goat. She wonders what the goat thinks of her. Can the goat tell, for example, that he is about to be killed in acknowledgement of her arrival in Africa? Can the goat, however, tell that she isn't directly complicit in the scheme? Can the goat fathom that she has never eaten an animal whose slaughter she'd witnessed?

Can the goat divine that all along she'd assumed the mutton chops she found so irresistible, the bacon that was the cornerstone of her weekend breakfast, the chicken breasts she found so wholesome – all of these things that she adored – came from some smart machine, and were not the result of horrific slaughter in dingy abattoirs?

Would the goat believe it if she said she thought highly of goats? That she found goats cuter and smarter than sheep because they are expressive, agile, worldly (they find their own food on cliff faces)?

She once saw a TV programme that claimed that animals could read the minds of human beings. But can this goat's supposed ability to read her mind atone for her impotence in the face of what is about to happen? Like the goat, she feels powerless, vanquished.

As if reading her thoughts of resignation, the goat bleats again. She thinks the sound it is making is: *Don't pull that Pontius Pilate shit on me, girl. Take a stand! When they came for the cow, you did the right thing by looking away. Those cows in America are artificially made anyway. So you ain't taking any life when you kill them. When they came for pigs, you did the right*

thing too by tucking into their bacon 'cos even Jesus hated pigs.
Now, they've come for the goat of Africa, take a stand, comrade –
after all, you're here to rediscover your roots. Take a stand and tell
them killing sacrificial goats is outdated in the Motherland!

The herb they'd made her inhale is playing tricks with her
mind. She takes solace in the fact that, even though she has
lost all ability to fight, the goat is still kicking wildly with its
legs, trying to break free. It hurls its head forwards, grazing
one of the boys holding it with its horns. The men, who've
been watching the scene with amusement, now move forwards, helping the boys subdue the goat. They pin it to the
ground once again. The animal bleats some more, a plaintive,
forlorn sound that brings tears to Fikile's eyes.

'Isn't there another way?' Fikile asks.

'No, this is what the ancestors require,' Bernard says. He
comes over carrying a huge white enamel basin, which he proceeds to place next to the goat's head. He accepts a big, shiny
knife from Auntie Promise. Fikile watches, as if in a trance, as
Bernard grabs the animal by one of its horns. Then his knife
starts shuttling back and forth around the animal's throat. There
is a hideous scream from the goat before the trachea breaks, and
torrents of blood come gushing out . . .

Fikile faints.

When Fikile comes to, the first thing she sees is a piece of the
dead goat's skin wrapped around her wrist, as if it were an
exotic bangle. She jumps up and screams, pulling at it.

'Easy now,' says Auntie Promise in a soothing voice. 'Take
it easy. The tough part of the ceremony is over. That piece of
goat skin on your wrist is called isiphandla. It's your amulet.

It's your protection against evil forces. You shall wear it at all times. It shall be there on your wrist until it disintegrates. The goat ceremony was simply to properly welcome you home, and introduce you to your ancestors seeing that when your parents had you in America, you were never introduced to your ancestors. You've never enjoyed ancestral protection all these years.'

'God in heaven! I didn't think you believed in that mumbo jumbo, Auntie. This ancestral worship shit is so unlike you . . .'

'No, my dear, we do not worship ancestors. We merely ask them to intercede on our behalf. For who are we to speak directly to God?'

Fikile is shivering all over. From shock or rage or cold, or all three. She does not answer her aunt.

'Some people ask their pastors to speak to God on their behalf. Others see Jesus as their connection to God. We are meek and humble enough to ask our ancestors, people we know and trust, to intercede on our behalf. Now we are fulfilling the imbeleko ceremony. You should know the word "imbeleko".'

Fikile sniffs. Her aunt knows very well that the chance of her, an American Zulu girl, knowing this obscure word is next to nil. Agitated, Fikile heaves to her feet, and marches away.

In the kitchen, Fikile does not find much solace. Some of the women, who turn out to be aunts and cousins of hers she's never been told about, are congregated there and try to make small talk. They speak in stilted English about their favourite TV shows, and the conversation veers to questions about Fikile's life in America.

'So, have you seen Nicki Minaj in the flesh?' a plump young woman asks.

'Is Pharrell really that beautiful, or is it TV make-believe?' another wants to know.

When, after a long while spent trying to answer their questions politely, someone asks, 'How does it feel living next door to Oprah?', she can't take their pointless chitchat any more.

Fikile walks back to the living room and finds her aunt sitting with Bernard on the couch. Fikile sees an empty bottle of Veuve Clicquot and a half-full one of Lagavulin. Her aunt must have brought it along.

'Bernard, I was telling this young American girl about my parents, her grandparents.' She does not look in the least bit phased by Fikile walking out on their conversation earlier.

'Painful as these things are, our children must know about them,' Bernard agrees.

'And this story will prepare her for South Africa. She will need to be strong if she's to survive in this country.'

'She's staying in this country?' Bernard is stunned. 'I thought she was just visiting, you know, to come and claim her birth right, her imbeleko.'

'No, she will be studying here.'

Fikile is glad that her aunt does not elaborate. Her mother had been struggling with depression since her father's unexpected death in a car accident and she was finally admitted to a mental hospital for help. Everyone thought it best that Fikile would come stay with her aunt and study here. Fikile does not know what Bernard would make of her mother's condition. He would probably say she needs spiritual cleansing or something.

'I must finish telling the story of my parents to my little niece now, Bernard,' Auntie Promise announces. 'And I'm telling the story in English – I hope you don't mind.'

'Not at all, Big Sister, not at all. I will sit and just listen. Maybe I will, in the process, learn how to tell a story in English. One never knows about these things.'

Auntie Promise takes over from where she left off. She says: 'Fikile, despite my age, I am still very much alert. Perhaps it is the nature of the story I am telling that keeps me alert. Perhaps, perhaps. But I remember quite distinctly that I got as far as the graveyard in the telling. The graveyard then we shall go back to. And what do we see? Multitudes of mourners were scattered all over Avalon Cemetery. The army and members of the police force had come out in numbers as well. But pay no mind to them now. Let us concentrate on our own little corner of the sprawling graveyard. Let us zoom in on two coffins. Two coffins sitting next to each other, two gaping holes waiting to receive them. The priest was reading from the holy book about long journeys travelled; about crossing the River Jordan. I'm recreating, even re-imagining these things now because, to be honest, I was only there at the graveyard physically. My mind was not there. It *couldn't* be there. I had run out of tears. I had exhausted the last remnants of my anger. My sadness was spent. I was just a zombie.

'I think it was at that stage that I was jerked out of my absent-mindedness. The priest told the men to start lowering the first coffin into the open grave. The rude thought was finally registering in my mind: my parents were truly going. I hadn't even looked at their faces, just one last time. I hadn't been able to bid them goodbye. Now their remains were about to be consigned to gaping holes. I had to see them, regardless of the ugliness of their faces in death. I wanted to see them. I was screaming now, "I want my mom . . . I want my mom!

Bloody boers, what did you do to my father? You will pay for this."

'Fikile, I am sitting with you now, more than twenty years after the fact. As if I don't feel the loss, the emptiness. I am sitting here, Fikile, looking back at my younger incarnation. My younger incarnation who was shouting and screaming. I am sitting here, surrounded by my loved ones, drinking good wine now, calm and collected, analysing. It seems all rosy now. But I am about to tell you something that will not make sense to you. Something that, today, still does not make sense even to me. I don't believe in so-called black magic. I know I shouldn't be saying this now, but many of the family rituals that I participate in do not make sense to me. But I still do them. My husband is a firm believer in these things, these spiritual things. My husband is a northerner, after all. Northerners believe you can send lightning to your enemy and kill them, if you want. They believe a lot of other things that you and I will regard as mumbo jumbo, right?

'Anyway, back to Avalon, back to the graveyard. The preacher man was droning on about ashes to ashes, dust to dust. Then the coffin started rocking. People paused to look at one another. Somebody said something about an earthquake. But the rocking and rattling of the coffin was gaining momentum. Then the lid flew open, breaking into splinters as if it had been struck by lightning. Logically by now we should have been running for our lives. But no, we stood and stared. As if hypnotised. *Run, run, run.* It was a repugnant thought throbbing inside my head. The idea of flight offended me because: how do I run away from my father when I haven't been able to lay my eyes on his face for one last time? When I haven't been able to look at him and mutter an apology about my long absence from home; when I haven't been able to sing him the final lullaby, recite poetry in his honour, shed tears that will bathe his face. But my other self was saying: *He's no longer your parent now. He is but a collection of charred remains. They reduced him and his wife to a mound of useless bones that should be disposed of. The sooner, the better.*

I hyperventilated and fainted right there. Everything that happened afterwards was told to me by the various relatives. Needless to say, there are discrepancies in the different versions.

'Some people said they saw a dove fly out of the coffin. Others say they simply heard a voice. And then there were those who swore they saw a skull jump out and speak in my father's voice. "Just what do you think you are doing?" it said. "Take us back home where we want to be left to rest. After all, that's where our hearts and souls are. Burying skeletons is pointless."

'Apparently people then ran helter-skelter. Only a few family members stayed behind, some of them tending to me as I lay unconscious. Alerted to the stampede, members of the police were approaching our section of the graveyard with their guns pointed, as if encircling a house where heavily armed terrorists are holed up.

'Word had travelled around the immediate vicinity of our own section of the graveyard. Now people who were busy with their own business at adjoining graves were running towards our graves. The various contingents of police scattered around Avalon got agitated. One of the officers in charge bellowed into a loudhailer, "People, people, State of Emergency regulations are still in force. If you start being disorderly, I shall order you to disperse. I repeat: if you start being disorderly, I shall order you to disperse. Bury your dead in peace and dignity, then go home. I repeat: stay in your section of the graveyard, bury your loved ones in peace and then go home."

'Order was eventually restored. People slunk back to their sections of the huge Avalon graveyard. But they kept taking quick, furtive glances in our direction. They were dying to see for themselves the coffin that had broken open. They were salivating at the prospect of sitting down at a shebeen later in the day, telling the story.

'Some would say they saw a white dove, others that they saw a skull jump from the coffin and speak. I can just picture them, moustaches of beer foam glinting from their upper lips. They would have taken their time to milk every bit and twist of the story, making it last, adding sugar and yeast to it, to make it bigger and sweeter, thus forcing listeners to keep buying beer after beer, so that the teller would relate every gory, bizarre detail.

'When I came to, our preacher man, stolid, calm and collected, had broken into song. Some of our party joined him. I could see one of my maternal uncles engaged in an agitated debate with relatives from my father's side.

'At long last, they seemed to have reached an agreement. The two coffins were loaded into the waiting hearses. Off we went. Back to Soweto. Back to this house, these premises. At some point, I fainted again. But the long and short of it is that the remains were finally interred here. Here, under the shade of the peach tree. Mind you, it is against municipal regulations to bury people in one's backyard. So, a few days later, municipal employees came here to try to carry out the township manager's instructions to remove the remains and transfer them to a government graveyard.

'No sooner had the municipal employees walked through the gate than a swarm of bees materialised out of nowhere. They descended on the municipal workers. There were screams as the men ran back to their truck. They drove away at high speed. One of them later died of bee stings. True story. Got printed in the *Sowetan*.

'A month later, another contingent of workers from the municipality came over. Some of the neighbours who had already come back to their houses saw the municipal truck park outside our yard. Word travels fast in the township. Soon, the neighbours were standing a safe distance from our house, others watching from the safety of their own yards. They knew they were in for some entertainment. It was a Friday afternoon, a hot summer day.

'Clearly, the municipal workers had not been apprised of what had happened to their colleagues a month earlier. They were singing and joshing around as they dragged their spades into the yard. As soon as the last man walked through the gate, the gate shut itself. But none of the workers noticed this, of course. Then a dark cloud took shape just above our yard. The men looked up, shook their heads and started digging. "Dig faster," the foreman said, "so we can all go home and drink beer. It's Friday, after all. Don't eat into my drinking time. Fast, fast, men!"

'But then, a bolt of lightning exploded out of the lone cloud hovering above the house. And, just like that, a flock of angry hadedahs – crying out, *nga-nga-nga-nga-nga* – descended on the men. Shrieking their war cry, *nga-nga-nga-nga*, and flapping their huge wings with fury, the birds attacked the men with their claws. *Nga-nga-nga-nga-nga-nga!* They deposited missiles of their shit on the men.

'Shocked, confused and scared, the men made for the gate. But it was locked. So they jumped over the fence. And, it was only then that they saw two huge white doves clobbering the windscreen of the truck with their super-strong beaks. Where was the foreman?

'The neighbours were no longer laughing. The truck's windscreen was a web of cracks. Police, in their warped assessment of things, might have accused the neighbours of stoning the truck. The municipal workers then saw the huge doves flying towards them, and they ran for their lives. Only much later, under police escort, did the driver of the truck come back to fetch the vehicle.

'Over the next few months, there were many bizarre attacks on municipal workers who visited the yard. Somebody with sense at the municipal offices must have decided enough was enough. So, for years, the house was left alone. After the political violence had abated, and Nelson Mandela was installed as the first democratically elected president of the country, more of the neighbours who had abandoned their houses came back. But only for a while. Every now and then a neighbour would complain about two doves accosting him at his gate, or depositing impossibly huge mounds of bird shit on his doorstep. Word soon got around: "Those are the doves from the Haunted House. The neighbourhood is getting punished for being complicit in the murder of those two old people those many years ago."

'Soon, the house and the street were the talking points at shebeens and in the pages of the new tabloid newspapers.

Schoolchildren have composed songs about it. This, then, is the story of my parents, dear Fikile.'

Fikile has goose bumps all over her arms by the time her aunt finishes the story. She doesn't know what to believe. 'So nobody stays in this house now?'

'No,' Auntie Promise says. 'We left the outside of the house as damaged as it was, didn't replace the windows. We repaired most of the inside, though, and the electricity, at first thinking that one of the family could live here. But we could not bring ourselves to do anything to the burnt-out bedroom. It is still exactly the way it was – I will not show you that room. But no one lives here. I had the fridge and stove-plate brought in for your ceremony.'

Her ceremony. Auntie Promise's story intrigued her so that she almost forgot about the whole ordeal. Well, at least it is all behind her now. She did what was expected of her and now everyone would leave her be.

'Some time ago, your father suggested that we turn the house into a museum,' Auntie Promise continues. 'But, hey, I don't know, I don't know. Where does one even begin? Your father would have been ideal to head that kind of project. Unfortunately, he had too many irons in the fire already. But it's an idea still worth pursuing.' She pauses to yawn. 'Yoh, I'm tired.'

'It's going to be a scary drive back home.' Fikile looks at the dark outside the windows.

'Who said anything about driving back? We are sleeping here. This is my home. This is where my umbilical cord is buried.'

'But I didn't bring my pyjamas, Auntie.'

'I had them packed in my bag while you were not looking.

I wanted our sleep-over to be the surprise it is turning out to be.'

Fikile feels a chill on the back of her neck. 'But, please, Auntie, we can't sleep here!'

'Why not?'

'Ghosts and stuff!'

'I thought you were a civilised American who didn't believe in that shit.'

'Auntie, it's just that this house feels . . . strange. And in any case, you said the bedroom is burnt out.'

'There is one more bedroom and there is the lounge. We are used to sleeping many family members to a single room. I shared with my siblings when we were little.'

The kitchen door opens. Fikile has been so engrossed in the story, she'd forgotten there were people busy around a fire outside. One of the young men comes in bearing a tray laden with what looks like dark oily tubes.

'Ah,' says Auntie Promise, 'the ceremonial meal is ready. You must pick the first piece since it was your ceremony.'

Fikile's stomach rumbles and she realises she is hungry. 'What is it?' she asks, reaching for the plate.

'It's the goat, of course. Well, the goat's intestines. You're going to eat the first piece, seeing as this is your goat.' Auntie Promise smiles.

Fikile shoots to her feet. 'No. I. Am. Not. Going. To. Do. That. I'm not doing that. Overmydeadbody!' She has never witnessed the slaughtering of any meat she's eaten and she is not about to start now.

'No ways am I eating this sh— No, I'm sorry, Auntie, but I can't.'

'You are not being asked; you're being told,' the young man with the tray says in perfect English.

Through the open door, a bird comes flying in in a flurry of feathers. It's one of the two huge doves. It settles itself next to the tray with the steaming mound of meat. It stares at Fikile with its red luminous eyes.

Tears fall from Fikile's eyes, and her hand trembles as she reaches for the piece of meat.

Beds Are Burning

Nomcebo was dismayed to find the front of her favourite butchery in Bramley all boarded up. She so wanted to buy fresh tripe! At least the butchers had had the foresight to indicate – with the aid of an elegantly printed flier pasted on what used to be the main door – where they'd moved. Hillbrow. That is where she would have to go, whether she liked it or not.

Chain stores such as Pick n Pay and Shoprite did sell tripe. But the problem with their stock of tripe was that it was bleached. What temerity!

She turned around and got back into her car, a BMW X5, one of the luxuries provided by her job as marketing director at a blue chip company. Another luxury was that she could take an afternoon off, like today, to sort out some personal admin. And to go buy her tripe.

She laughed when she thought what some of her colleagues would say about her love for tripe.

In their twangy accents, they would say: *That Nomcebo, she's educated, I mean she has three degrees, for goodness sake – she's moneyed, well travelled and open-minded. She possesses many other attributes of a reasonable and civilised person, but, can you believe it, she loves tripe. And not the bleached type they sell in the supermarkets – she likes it in that green-black colour. Yuck!*

As far as Nomcebo was concerned, you could clean tripe for hygienic purposes; you could package it glamorously; you could market it whichever way you want to upmarket consumers; you could call it exotic names – 'mala mogodu', 'itwani', 'upense', or whatever tickles your fancy. But for crying in a bucket, don't pulverise the darn thing by soaking it in bleach. When you do that, it turns completely white and textureless. With the colour gone, the funk is gone; the grit is gone; the grease is gone. And with the funk and the grit and the grease gone, the flavour is gone! So, what's the point? Might as well eat bleached dishwashing rags and bleached veggies!

Nomcebo was so determined to prepare a dish of proper tripe for dinner, she did not mind driving up the busy Louis Botha Avenue, all the way to Hillbrow to the butchery's new location. Tripe and dumplings, ahhhhh . . .

A weekday, Hillbrow was not as hectic as it would have been on a Saturday or Sunday. But it still was busy, and uncomfortable to drive in. And here she was, all because of her need for green-black, real McCoy tripe.

She was lucky to find parking at the corner of Edith Cavell and Pretoria Streets. As soon as she opened her car door, Hillbrow announced itself in its smells, noises, sights. There was the cloying putrescence of cooking oil that had been used over and over again to fry Russians, chips, fish and whatever. The aroma of roasted maize. The stench of stale urine, the sour odour of sewage. The smell of exhaust fumes. And, yes, if you had a particularly keen sense of smell, you would think the place smelt like one huge human armpit.

A fruit-and-vegetable vendor was standing proudly behind her trestle table. On the table: oranges arranged in neat pyramids of four. Peaches, also in pyramids, wearing golden smiles. Nectarines blushing. Tomatoes red and plump. Green peppers, red peppers, yellow peppers. Bananas a ripe yellow. Plums dark and tempting. Chillies green and red, full of menace. Spinach lush and dark green. Grapes black and white, glistening with dew – recently rescued from a cooler box at the vendor's feet. Pears, madumbe, yams, coconut, cabbages, green beans, carrots.

A waif of a woman in an oversized dress shouted, 'Get your vuvuzela today!', before she handed out handbills with the words: *Revolutionary Penis ENLARGER. Holesome good fun.*

A young man shouted, 'Here's something hard you've been looking for', before he gave passers-by a flyer with the words: *Ghetto Viagra. Hard Times Have Never Been So Good.*

A man bellowed: 'Prophet Dr Abdul Karanga Abduraman, all the way from Malawi. Will heal any illness. Will bring peace and prosperity to your house!'

A young man screamed: 'Out of work? Need a lawyer? Phone this number.' And he would hand you a handbill with the words: *SMART LEGAL EAGLE – PHONE NOW.*

Another young man: 'Get your Lotto tickets today. Ten-million-rand jackpot this Saturday. Don't say I didn't tell you! Get your Lotto tickets now!'

There were the inevitable police and fire-brigade sirens that one associates with a big city; the screeching of car tyres; the honking horns; the loud music banging from expensive speakers.

Handbag clasped in one hand, Nomcebo locked her car, and walked towards the pedestrian crossing. She had settled for a smart-casual look for the day: a bright-green sleeveless, knee-length wrap-around African costume. It had subtle off-white floral patterns. The dress hugged her breasts, and emphasised

131

her curves. She had on a matching turban, and high-heeled shoes designed by Keke, the shoemaker who was making a name for himself in Johannesburg. The necklace was of tiny seashells strung on a genuine gold chain, with a huge copper pendant in the form of the map of the continent. Her handbag was genuine leather, but also in matching green.

Nomcebo passed a group of five male street sweepers and stood at the corner of the street, waiting for the pedestrian light to turn green.

'Jesus on the cross, look at those legs. She must be a dancer of sorts,' she heard one of the street sweepers behind her say in Zulu.

'Oh, boy, I bet you she can dance,' said another one. 'Did you see those watermelons jiggling as she moved. They go one-two, I-love-you; three-four, I-want-you!'

'Damn, you guys don't have eyes,' a third jumped in. 'Look at the contours of her booty. Can even tell she's wearing a G-string. See how the G-string slices the big mountain of her behind into two hillocks. Yerrrh, Joe! Give me one night with her. Just one night, my bro – she won't be going back to Congo in a hurry.'

This elicited exclamations of protest. 'No, she's too light to be from Congo! Maybe from some other African country. How about Angola? They've got some light-complexioned sisters there. Mulatto. Light just like our own coloureds.'

'Nah, but that woman there isn't from Congo, not from Angola, not from anywhere else but Nigeria.'

'Naw, man, they got dark sisters in Nigeria. Dark and muscular and aggressive, like. That sister over there is smooth and tender like a ripe peach, no?'

Nomcebo looked straight ahead as if she couldn't hear, or understand them. They went on and on:

'I'll tell you something,' one man said, 'those clothes she's wearing, that's the Nigerian national colour, the green she is wearing.'

'Shit, then she must be a drug dealer,' another exclaimed. 'Did you see the wheels she's cruising in? A sleek BMW X5, my brother. But still, that ezi of hers is worth exploring. When I get between those hillocks she's dragging, hhhmm, weh mame! She'll forget she comes from Lagos.'

Only then did someone consider the possibility that she might be listening: 'Don't speak too loudly – maybe she can understand us.'

'Nah, you can tell she speaks some shalambombo, doesn't understand our local languages.'

'You'll be surprised. These foreigners pick up our languages sharp-sharp, just like that.'

'No, she's too top-shayela to care about local languages. It's the starving foreigners, the ones at the bottom of the feeding chain, who feel obliged to learn local languages – just in order to survive in this tough country of ours. But whether she can understand us or not, I wouldn't mind exploring her . . .'

'Then stop irritating us. She's right here in front of you. Speak to her. She won't bite. At least I don't think she will.'

'Seek ye the legs, brothers. Seek ye the legs. Puh-raise the Lord. Ah, the legs. The legs of thunder.'

Nomcebo wished the light would turn green now. What was taking so long?

Then she heard a new voice, one of the street sweepers who hadn't spoken before. His voice was tremulous, and deep like a bass drum. It said, 'Can't believe you guys are so down in the gutter you're heaping compliments upon a frigging kwere-kwere. These kwerekweres, these things smell. They bring diseases. They live the life of corruption and damnation. They steal . . .'

The light turned green. Nomcebo crossed the road, anger simmering inside her.

She moved her shoulders as if to shake off the men's words as she entered the butchery. She wouldn't let it get to her.

The smile of her butcher, Imraan, greeted her as she walked in, making her feel much better. Imraan had become a friend over the years, and he was happy she had not had any difficulty finding the new premises. She bought tripe, including lamb liver, ox tongue and ox kidneys.

'Any lamb chops for you, my sister?' asked the man serving her. 'We have some top-class grass-fed beef from Botswana. Top-notch steaks there. We also have exquisite boerewors from the Karoo.'

'No, thanks, my home freezer is full to bursting. Meat for Africa. And our friends in Iraq and Afghanistan. All I want today is tripe.'

'You can't walk into an Indian-owned business and not buy more!' said Imraan, the butcher, adjusting his kufi. 'Such an Indian salesman would have a fatwa declared on him. We were put on this planet to sell things. By any means necessary.'

'On second thoughts, I will have four kilograms of lamb chops.' Where was she going to keep all this meat? She decided she would transfer some of it to her in-laws' freezer, which was much bigger and almost always half-empty.

'Themba,' Imraan said to the young man serving Nomcebo,

'give the lady some bonsella. She's a regular, you know. Give her a kilogram of biltong. By any means necessary.'

Imraan was such a persuasive salesman that she ended up buying enough food for a big party. She thanked them for the complimentary biltong, paid for her goodies, said her goodbyes. Once outside the butchery, she walked towards where she'd parked. Waiting for the light to turn green, she noticed that the street sweepers were still there on the opposite corner, smoking cigarettes. She hoped to God they were not going to start on her again. The robot turned green. She started walking.

'Speak to her, Joe,' one of them spoke in urgent tones to his friend. 'Speak to her before she drives off. Can't wait to have a friend who goes out with a foreigner. Interested to know what a foreigner tastes like.'

Still speaking in Zulu, another one said, 'Joe, don't waste your time on this disease carrier.' Then he switched to heavily accented English, addressing Nomcebo: 'Hey, you, when you gone home?'

'What did you say?' Nomcebo responded in English, her sing-song accent oozing sophistication. 'Are you talking to me by any chance?'

'Yes, who do you think? You go home now. Back home Nigeria, or Congo, or wherever you come from. Your father Mandela, he dead; you foreigners go home now. Mandela, he allow you come here and steal our jobs, and make our city dirty. Look, we sweep a street while you drive goma-goma fancy BMW. Maybe you even work in air-condition office. Live in suburb while we live in shacks. You steal everything from us. Your childrens, dey go to fancy school, while ours no school coz we can't pay. Where you even get de money?'

Nomcebo opened her mouth to answer, but he went right on with his tirade: 'Is ovias. You pump drugs onto our streets. Das how you make your money. You kill our childrens.' Flecks of foam had formed at the corners of his mouth. He continued, 'You stinking. Das why I don't cry when dey attack you. And you call it zenofobis. Is no zenofobis. Is no zenofobis about it. Is de truth truth. Our people, dey are tired. Tired! Time to go home. Will help you carry your suitcases to airport, to train station, to bus station. To wherever. As long as you leave our country. Enough. And you leave that BMW behind, coz where you come from you don't even have roads.'

Nomcebo had had enough. 'Hheyi, webhuti, ungabhoshi ngomlomo!' she shrieked, telling him to stop defecating through his mouth. 'Ubobakhetha abantu, careful who you talk to.'

Passers-by stopped to stare. One of the street sweepers said, 'Hhawu, she speaks top-notch Zulu, just like they speak it in Zululand. Did you hear her?'

The man who had addressed her directly faltered, but soon regained his composure. Now he said to her in Zulu, 'Sisi wami, listen, in these times you must stop dressing like the kwere-kweres. Otherwise you'll get mistaken for one and . . .' He left it hanging.

'Hheyi, webhuti, I will dress the way I feel, the way I like,' said Nomcebo, opening her car door, dumping her handbag and bags of meat before closing the door again. She wasn't ready yet to go home. The men had defiled her and now she had to deal with them. Once and for all. She was going to 'tell them cash'. Yes, she was familiar with the township slang.

'Oh,' said the angry man, 'now I can see what you are. You are one of the local whores who sleep with foreigners. And they buy you fancy cars, and then you think you're better than us. Bloody gold digger.'

The man wasn't looking at her as he spoke, taking a lit cigarette from his friend to drag on. He did not see that Nomcebo was putting one foot before the other, gaining on him. On uttering his last phrase – 'bloody gold digger' – Nomcebo punched him hard in the mouth.

'I'll make you eat beetroot, you fool,' she said. While he was still recovering from the shock of 'beetroot' – blood and loose teeth – Nomcebo took off her high-heeled shoe, and started clobbering him. A crowd of onlookers had gathered.

'Mshaye, beat him up,' screamed a woman. 'Mshaye udoti! Washaye amasende!'

Soon, more women were screaming: 'Mshaye!'

Some male onlookers were laughing. One said, 'That fool never herded cattle when he was a boy! He never did stick fighting with other boys. He is as soft as rotten tomatoes. How can you even bleed from a woman's punch?'

A woman shouted from the throng, berating them for simply looking on as Nomcebo beat the man: 'Hhawu, nathula ikwerekwere lishaya indoda yomuntu!'

'She is South African, not a kwerekwere,' someone corrected the woman.

'If she's a South African,' said the woman, 'then she must be one of those who sleep with foreigners. Look at how she's dressed! A woman does not fight with a man in the street. Never!'

Attracted by the crowd, a Metro cop who had been driving past stopped his car and came running to the scene.

'What's happening here?' he asked, looking at the man whose head was bleeding, sprawled on the pavement. Then the policeman looked at Nomcebo and spoke to her: 'What happened?'

Nomcebo, who was still barefoot, took her time to relate the story to the policeman in English.

The policeman checked on the man on the ground and helped him up. Then he turned to the crowd. 'Okay, everybody, move on. The movie is over. Move on before I arrest you. Move on.' Some people moved; others shuffled their feet without moving.

He turned to Nomcebo: 'Okay, I hear your story. But are you sure you're not a foreigner?'

'What do you mean?'

'You speak English in a funny way. Yes, you do. That's what I said. Let me see your papers, please. Your identification papers.'

Nomcebo sighed. Speaking in Zulu in a deep rural accent that she knew drove the fear of God into the hearts of city-born people, she said, 'Hhayi-ke, shem. I think you too want to taste my high-heeled shoe. I will give you a taste, just a tiny taste, and then I'll phone your boss, Wilton Venter.' She invoked the name of the chief of the Metro Police whom she had met at a function a few weeks ago. 'Would you like me to do that,' she looked at his name badge, 'Would you like me to do that, Officer Motaung? Would you like me to give you a taste of my shoe before I phone your boss?'

The policeman seemed stunned. But he soon recovered. He said, 'But, such a beautiful lady like you, beating up people in the street . . . It's so uncivilised and unladylike. That's what I said. What's wrong, my dear? Are you somehow stressed?'

'But I told you he started it! I have witnesses.' Nomcebo sat down on the pavement to put on her shoes. The hem of her dress rode a few centimetres up her thighs.

'Puh-raise the Lord. Sweet Jesus on the cross!' sang one of the street sweepers who had ignored the order to disperse. 'Leg bone connected to the knee bone, and the knee bone connected to the thigh bone, and the thigh led to the Kingdom of the Lord.'

The remaining onlookers who'd heard the corrupted version of the famous American spiritual laughed. Nomcebo covered her thighs.

A vendor woman screamed from across the road: 'Hhayi bo! Mr Phoyisa, leave that woman alone. These men started the trouble. They asked for it. You can't arrest her.'

'I am going to arrest you for public disturbance; that's what I said,' the policeman shouted back at her.

'No, no, no, Mr Policeman!' shouted another woman. 'She might be kwerekwere, but she's still a woman. Women are tired of abuse. Rhaaa!'

The policeman shook his head. He refocused his attention on Nomcebo. He said, 'My darling sister, I think you need a gentleman like myself. Yes, you do.' He played with his well-groomed moustache. 'I can see you're sleeping with a foreigner. That, I am positive about. I can smell it in the air.' He sniffed. 'See, my darling sister, there's no shortage of gentlemen in this country; no, there isn't. That's what I said. It's just that you've been looking in all the wrong places. And that's God's truth. All the wrong places.'

'You're right about one thing. Yes, I am married to a Nigerian . . .'

'How can you do that to us, my sister? Is he rich? Is he the one who taught you to beat up men? Our women don't do that; no, they don't. It's only those who go out with foreigners who do that. Uh-huh, that's what I said. They've lost their moral compass. The moral compass is what they've lost, that's what I said.'

'I don't believe this,' said Nomcebo, and started walking towards her car.

The policeman followed her to her car, speaking in a calming tone: 'My sister, these foreigners are destroying our country. And you are helping them; yes, you are. But let me warn you. As a policeman who patrols this city, somebody told me there's a plan afoot to purge our city of these foreigners. Especially your Nigerians. Better choose sides now, before it's too late.'

Nomcebo spat at the policeman's shoes, turned on her heel, got into her car and drove off.

A week later, Nomcebo would recall the policeman's warning when she was reading the news of what happened at Holyfire Overflow Ministries Church. From the article she was breathlessly reading in bed, Nomcebo gathered a few facts about this church: it was one of hundreds of Pentecostal churches that had mushroomed in the Johannesburg inner-city from the time the country's borders opened up to an influx of foreigners from up north. It drew its congregants from the West African community – mainly Nigerians and Ghanaians.

The church distinguished itself from its competitors – yes, ministers at these born-again churches were not shy to point out that they were competing for the souls of would-be congregants – simply through the premises it occupied. It was housed in a building that used to be a synagogue, at the corner of Grafton and Rockey Streets. *Church Massacre* – this was the headline that had drawn Nomcebo to the article in the first place. It was a short piece, just uploaded to the newspaper's online site. As she raced towards the end of the story, she kept muttering, 'Oh, my God, Yeoville. Yeoville.' Some of the ladies she had met at the United Nigerian Wives in South Africa lived in Yeoville. Some in Hillbrow, others in Berea. As far as she could recall, many of them were quite religious. Logically, some of them would be familiar with this church. They might even be members. And now . . . they might even be injured or worse!

She flung the paper on the floor and reached for her cellphone. She quickly dialled the number of Sarah Onisola, the lady who'd introduced her to the rest of the members of Unwisa. 'Come on, pick up. Pick up, dammit!'

Emeka, who was sleeping next to her, trying to recover from a hangover, mumbled a complaint: 'Can't a person sleep in peace, even on God's day of rest?'

Nomcebo was still pacing up and down as the phone rang a number of times before it went to voice mail. She left an urgent call-back message.

Then she dialled Sibongile, one of the Unwise members. No response. She rushed to the bathroom, brushed her teeth, considered taking a shower. Decided against it. She had to drive to Sarah's place right away. Or even make a turn in Yeoville, speak to people at the police station, interview neighbours, anything. It had to happen now. No time to lose. The latent journalist in her was on her feet. And the activist too.

Back in the bedroom, she shed her pyjamas, put on a clean pair of panties and clambered into a pair of jeans.

'Whoa, lady, whoa, what's the rush?' Emeka was sitting up, staring at her. 'Who has died that you must leave the house without even taking a shower?'

'Read the paper – online,' she panted, as she ran to her walk-in closet and started pawing her mound of neatly ironed T-shirts in one of the compartments of her elaborately designed closet.

'Shat,' he murmured as he read the story on his iPad. 'Who does this? What kind of creature does this?'

He flung the paper on the floor, and said, 'So, what's the plan? Where you goin'?'

'One of those killed could be one of my friends.'

'You have friends in Yeoville, Hillbrow? That's news to me.' She'd never told him about her involvement in United Nigerian Wives in South Africa because she didn't want him to know that she was sometimes harassed for being married to a Nigerian man and needed a support group. She didn't want him to worry. He didn't even know that she blogged about her experiences. And because he was not on Facebook, preferring Twitter, he was in no position to know what she posted on her page.

'This is no time for talking. I have to go, baby.'

'No, you can't do that. No woman of mine is going there. The attack could lead to counter-attacks, you know how these things are. And—'

'I have to know that my friends are safe.' Breathe. 'Or even still alive.'

'Okay, but let's first check social media and see if there are new developments. That's the beauty of Twitter – always fresh and up to date. What I'm sayin', sweetie, is before you drive over there, let's make sure you don't get caught in some crossfire.'

He opened Twitter on his iPad.

Having recovered from her initial shock, Nomcebo decided to take a swift shower after all. She couldn't go around harassing people with her bodily odours. While Emeka scrolled through tweets, she rushed to the bathroom.

'Oh, hell! Motherfucking shit!'

Even above the hiss of the shower, she could hear Emeka shouting in disbelief. She finished quickly, towelled off and rushed back to the bedroom.

'What is it, sweetie? Speak to me, what's happening?'

'Baby, you ain't goin' to no Yeoville, no way. Who does this to a fellow human being? My wife can't get entangled in this shit.'

'Give me that iPad!'

He tried to shield the device behind his back. 'No, you won't be able to handle this shit, baby. You won't.'

'What is it? Let me see for myself. You are not my nanny. I am a grown-ass woman, dammit. Let me see!'

There were tears in his eyes. Nomcebo used this moment of weakness to snatch the iPad away from him. She saw that he had YouTube open.

Nomcebo sat on the lounge chair across from the bed, and played the YouTube footage Emeka had just watched.

The opening frame shows the exterior of what looks like a synagogue. You can hear background noises – cars driving past, the hubbub of voices. A group of men, with their backs to the camera, moves steadily towards the entrance. They are wearing heavy coats, heads covered in skullcaps, hats. The cameraman, who seems to know what he is doing, then zooms in on the main door.

A voice says: *What are you waiting for?*

One of the men kicks the door open, the camera capturing the action expertly.

From the bouncing movements of his camera, you can tell the cameraman is jogging towards the door. But he is firmly in control. You can see that, too.

There are throngs of people inside the building. The unmistakable sound of gunfire can be heard. One shot, two. Screams. And then a voice, sounding distant but intelligible: *No one leaves this place until we are done with you.*

More screams. A stampede. Another gun shot. Then silence.

The commanding voice again: *Everybody flat on their stomachs.*

The camera sweeps across the cavernous interior. People lying on the floor, crouching behind benches. Silence.

And then the commanding voice: *Phezu kwabo – get them!*

Somebody giggles (probably the cameraman because the sound is quite distinct). Then the camera shows the men in heavy coats pouncing, with an assortment of weapons, on the cowering people – men, women, children. Screams ring out.

The camera zooms in on a machete as it slices open the head of a man. A club smashes the head of a woman. More screams.

Every time somebody tries to get up, the camera zooms in on them. The cameraman shouts: *Get that one who's trying to get away. Yeah, the red jersey over there.*

The man in the red jersey is scrambling for a nearby window, but one of the assailants plunges a huge knife into his side. Red Jersey slithers against the wall, collapses on the floor. The camera stays with him for a while, zooming in on his face. His eyes are wide. Then they start fading. The camera stays with him until the eyes are tight. Then the camera does a wide sweep of mayhem in the church.

The murderers seem unhurried. Precise. Calculated. Vicious.

The voice of the commander is heard not too far from the camera: *My dear reverend, sing 'The Lord is my Shepherd'. Sing for your people! They need the soothing words of that psalm. Sing it, my dear reverend.* The voice sounds almost sincere, even sympathetic.

The cameraman giggles, says: *Look at the fucking kwerekwere, he must have shat himself by now!* His camera sweeps to the pulpit, and he does an impressive close-up of the pastor's sweating face as the man sings: *'The Lord is my shepherd; I shall not want. He maketh me to lie down . . .'*

A scream so piercing it almost makes the windows shudder . . .

'He maketh me to lie down in green pastures: He leadeth me beside the still waters.'

The thud of a club against human bone. A weak moan.

'He restoreth my soul: He leadeth me in the paths of righteousness for His name's sake . . .'

A wail, a plea for mercy.

'Yea, though I walk through the valley of the shadow of death, I will fear no evil: for Thou art with me; Thy rod and Thy staff, they comfort me . . .'

A woman screams: *You've killed my baby!*

A cracking thud and she is silent.

'Thou preparest a table before me in the presence of mine enemies: Thou anointest my head with oil; my cup runneth over . . .'

A loud guffaw from the cameraman as he turns away from the pastor and zooms in on one of the armed men, who is ripping the clothes off a teenage girl.

'Surely goodness and mercy shall follow me all the days of my life: and I will dwell in the house of the Lord for ever.'

Nomcebo put the iPad down, weeping, her shoulders shaking. Emeka got up and sat by her side, cradling her head against his chest, massaging her back. For a long time they just sat there, rocking back and forth.

'I need to check on my family,' Emeka said and took his phone. He started typing a message.

'We should go to them,' Nomcebo said. 'We should go be with them.'

They wordlessly left the house. Drove with the radio off. They were soon on the concrete freeway, towards Montecasino. Before they knew it, they were at his parents' house in Douglasdale.

The mood at the house was sombre. All through the day, Emeka's father's friends and acquaintances, all foreign nationals, started drifting in.

Nomcebo's phone rang. It was Sarah Onisola. She picked up. 'Nomcebo, thanks for checking on us earlier today.'

'I'm glad you got my message. Thank goodness you're okay.'

'Yes, thank God. I checked with all the girls in the group; sounds like our inner circle is still intact, but about four of our distant friends were at the church. One of them was killed, the others survived, and are still in hospital.'

They spoke some more. Nomcebo rang off.

The meat Nomcebo had bought two weeks ago at the butcher in Hillbrow, and which she'd stored in her in-laws' freezer, now came in handy. Food was prepared for everyone. There was the extra tripe she had bought as well. But, for the first time in her life, Nomcebo did not find the sight of the cooking tripe appetising. And when she helped to cut up some of the red meat, the bloodiness of it made her nauseous. Her mind flashed to the YouTube video and she went to the bathroom to hide her teary eyes.

That evening, the Okparas and their friends huddled around the TV and listened to the latest dispatch. Attacks against foreigners – mainly Somalis and Pakistanis – had been reported in townships across the greater Johannesburg metro area. There were also sporadic explosions in Port Elizabeth, East London, Cape Town.

Emeka spoke to no one in particular: 'Ain't no point in talkin' about what caused this madness. Point now is: what do we do? How do we respond? How do we reverse the damage? That video was uploaded to an anonymous YouTube channel, so I don't expect anyone will take responsibility for the heinous act. We at least have to set our own tone to the madness. Know wha' I'm sayin'?'

He looked around the lounge, and when no one responded, added: 'Let's take them head on.'

A gasp went up among the small gathered group.

He held up his hands to reassure them he wasn't finished: 'When I say let's take them on, I don't mean violently. Nothing can be gained from such a proposition. What I mean is, let's do something that will make them realise we aren't going anywhere! We aren't cowed by their brutality. We are here to stay, and we are willing to work, and live cheek by jowl with those South Africans who recognise our humanity. And I know I am speaking about the majority of South Africans here.' He got up and stood in front of the television, facing them. 'Let me tell you, friends, I have been in this country long enough to see the bottomless reservoir of goodwill and spirit of neighbourliness. But, as in any country, all over the world, there are also pockets of evil. Mark my words, I said *pockets* of evil. Versus oceans of goodwill.' He started pacing up and down, all the while addressing those congregated. 'Let us, through whatever action we take now, tap into those reservoirs of goodwill. Let us work with the positive, progressive forces and spite the evil ones who are not sustainable anyway. We know we shall win as we are confident of good over evil, as Bob Marley said. This attack on our people is a call to action. Let us stand up to be counted. Let us not shrink back into our cocoons of fear and complacency. Let us move forward . . .'

Silence in the room. While Emeka paused, his father cleared his throat loudly. Emeka looked at him, nodded. His father said: 'I never knew we had a preacher in the Okpara family.' He paused to allow the nervous laughter, then continued: 'The young man has spoken with such passion and conviction. But please clarify what you mean, my boy. What kind of action did you have in mind that will make them realise we are serious about staying here, without coming across as being arrogant and warlike?'

Before Emeka could respond, Nomcebo jumped up and blurted out: 'We could go to the radio stations, TV channels and newspapers, and condemn this in the strongest terms possible. But that is only too predictable. I am sure somebody has already spoken to the media, and the outcome of such condemnation will be in the newspapers tomorrow. We need something to get the country, the world, even, to sit up and listen.'

She paused. A woman whispered to a friend: 'Isn't she a South African? What's she doing here; what does she know about our problems?'

Professor Okpara turned to the two women and said something in Igbo, something that made the women, and some men, nod and take a fresh look at Nomcebo.

'As a South African, I might be part of the problem; or at least some might perceive me as part of the problem. Be that as it may, I think I have something that will prove to be a major contribution to the resolution of this problem. The divide between locals and foreigners has been there as far back as 1994 when our borders opened up. But our elders decided to assume the ostrich stance. And I am talking about both local and foreign elders, some of whom went to university together beyond the borders of this country. What we've never had is a proper dialogue. Our local brothers have failed to make the foreigners feel welcome here; and the foreigners have never made any attempt to start a dialogue with locals. If we did speak to each other, we chose to speak *past* each other. We criticised each other. Each side boasted how much better educated, or how well travelled, or how very "civilised" they were . . .'

There were murmurs from the audience, the shuffling of feet.

A man who had been shaking his head couldn't restrain himself any longer: 'Look, in Naija we opened our borders for South African businessmen; we gave them trading licences. And when our own businessmen come here, you stop them at the airport. You ask them to produce stupid yellow fever certificates.'

A woman clapped her hands, and said, 'And they thought we couldn't play that game. We stopped them at our airport as well, asked them for yellow fever certificates. These South Africans, mnnccccm! They think we don't know these games—'

'Order, Madame Obaigbena, order please,' said Professor Okpara.

This seemed to fuel Madame Obaigbena to explain: 'We been playin' these games at the highes' level. With the arrogan' Europeans and Americans. And who do these South Africans think they be? Stupid Johnny-come-latelies in international affairs. United Nations? We been there as a liberated African country. Organisation o' African Unity, we birthed that ting. We the aristocrafts o' international diplomacy. Aristocrafts o' African liberation. Where they been? For a long time we let them fool theyselves to tink they the biggest economy on thi' continent. Me, I tell you, we tired of their nonsense. We've reclaim our title. Me, I tell you, Naija number one on this continent. No contes'. Mnncccm.'

'My sister, we know you're hurting. We're mourning the deaths of some of our countrymen,' said Mrs Okpara. 'Let the pain we feel inside not cloud our judgment, and displace our energy and focus.'

'Who you? You not even from Naija, you West Indian coconut, you. Just because you married our brother Professor Okpara doesn't make you betta than the rest of other stupid Wes' Indians,' said Mrs Obaigbena. 'What you Wes' Indians kno' about fighting? About oil? All you know is rum and rice. Thas all you kno'. And you sleep under a tree, until you get woken up by a fallin' coconut hittin' your head. You get smacked in yo head too many times, you get dumb. Me I'm a tell you!'

'Sister Obaigbena,' a respectable-looking woman begged, 'please keep quiet.'

'Oh, I must keep quiet-o! Jus' because I don' have the title "Professor" before my name? Tell you what, all of you combined, you do not have the title "Billionaire". Even if you take all your annual professorial peanuts, which you call salaries.

Multiply that by the next ten years, add your pensions, your life savings, the shacks you mistake for houses, you still will never earn the title "Billionaire" before your name! Me, I'm a tell you. I'm a billionaire. Everybody in Naija knows me, eheh . . .'

Professor Okpara moved decisively and marshalled the unruly woman out of the room. She tried to resist. In the scuffle that ensued, a bottle slid out of her handbag and shattered on the tiled floor. The room was suddenly suffused with the smell of expensive gin.

As she was being led away, she shrieked, 'In Naija we buy our gin from London, that's what we do. We are not cheapos. And we go to Switzerland to look at the white folks skiing. And we say to them: "Ah, who is the monkey now? Dance and spin and twirl about, monkeys." Those Europeans, they like our money; they keep it safe for us.'

Nomcebo, who was in tears now, said, 'People, I fully appreciate we are all hurting. But what happened to Clement Emekensha, who was beaten up and stripped naked by police in Cape Town for the simple reason he's Nigerian, will happen again if we don't stand together and take decisive action.'

'Yes!' the people before her shouted.

'What happened to Ernesto Alfabeto Nhamuave, who was burnt alive by ordinary South Africans for simply being Mozambican, will happen again if we don't act.'

'Damn barbarians!'

'What happened at that church in Yeoville will keep recurring if we continue throwing abuse at each other instead of standing together!'

'Say it again!'

'The unreported indignities visited on foreign nationals in

this country will be a daily occurrence if we are not seen to be stemming this tide through decisive action.'

'Decisive action!'

'Here me speak, people, here me speak. Don't just shake your heads in agreement before you've even heard what I have to say.' She paused. 'The loudest message we can put across right now can be through a protest march.'

'Oh, no, you South Africans and protest marches . . .' someone muttered.

'Hear me out, hear me out! We don't just stage a march for the sake of staging a march. We march on the headquarters of the ruling party in town.'

'They'll shoot us down!'

Nomcebo's organisational skills as a marketing director were coming to the fore. 'Many of those people at headquarters will be receptive to the message. Many of them, as we know, were benefactors of the hospitality not only of Nigerians during apartheid, but they were also hosted by many countries whose foreign nationals now stay in South Africa. Those people at headquarters were refugees in Angola, Mozambique, Tanzania, Uganda. You name it. Some of these ANC officials even have foreign wives and children who were born in foreign climes. My own father is a powerful man at Luthuli House. A tried-and-tested fighter.'

'Told you she was a spy,' a woman murmured to a friend. 'Here to derail our efforts.'

Nomcebo continued, 'But I am not speaking here on my father's behalf, or on behalf of Luthuli House per se. All I'm trying to illustrate is this: the march will be disciplined, will be done out of respect. And will receive a sympathetic hearing from people who matter, people who can make a change, and it will be joined by thousands of sympathetic South Africans. And we know they are in the majority, like my husband, Emeka, said.'

She smiled at Emeka, who moved closer to her and took her hand.

'Like all legal protest activities, the march will be escorted by the Metro Police,' she said. 'Oh, yes, we will not try to cut corners. We are going to apply for permission to march to show our respect for the country's laws, and our faith in the city administration. We have to do things the proper way to get respect from people who matter; and from the larger South African populace, most of whom don't fully understand what we, the foreign nationals, are all about.'

She could see that the people before her were still sceptical. She wished this was as easy as taking off her shoe and clobbering a xenophobic street sweeper, but quick satisfaction, violence, would only make matters worse and turn people against them. 'Yes, the changes in attitude and behaviour will not happen overnight,' she agreed, 'but the march and the presentation of a memorandum to authorities in government will make people sit up and take notice. Most importantly, those who have been apathetic so far will think hard about the future implications of these confrontations and tensions between people who, for all intents and purposes, are simply trying to get on with their lives.'

Now she had them in the palm of her hands.

She continued, 'From marching on the headquarters, we then go and present a strong petition to the Nigerian consulate, requesting them to call for an urgent meeting with representatives from the South African foreign affairs department. These will not be isolated incidents, but a build-up of a momentous movement to put this matter on the centre stage of diplomatic interactions between South Africa and the governments represented in this country.'

After Nomcebo's impromptu speech, some elders – including Professor Okpara and the president of a new organisation called the Nigerian Union in South Africa – stood apart and began drawing up a concrete programme of action, and allocating responsibilities to individuals, based on their strengths, experience and networking capabilities.

'And I think we can invite the leadership of student organisations for foreign nationals at the various universities,' said Nomcebo. 'And we need the president of the United Nigerian Wives in South Africa to be part of this organising committee.'

'Nigerian Wives what?' asked Professor Okpara.

'Daddy,' she responded, 'it's an organisation of local women married to Nigerian guys.'

'How the hell do you know all these organisations?' asked Emeka.

'The internet, baba, the internet,' she said. 'Also, as a marketer, I get to sit in on all these focus groups whenever we are trying out a new product on the targeted market. And, through these focus groups, one gets to interact with all sorts of people.'

Emeka exchanged glances with his father and the others in the tight interim organising group.

'But you gotta be careful of these online organisations,' said Professor Okpara. 'You see, in Nigeria, a supposed organisation often turns out to consist of only one person. These days, a Nigerian with a cause will simply start a church . . .' The professor looked around conspiratorially before he said, 'I know that Mrs Obaigbena runs two churches in Lagos, one in Abuja and another one in Delta State somewhere. Yes, it's true she pays university fees for many Nigerian kids. But she also collects lots of money through the churches. It is also at these churches that she sells some of her many short-lived, cause-driven newspapers and pamphlets.'

With the responsibilities and tasks having been allocated to the relevant people, the men retired to the lounge where they had cognac and whisky. The women congregated around the dining room and drank wine. Mrs Obaigbena was snoring from a sofa in the long corridor linking the dining room with the lounge.

Much later, Nomcebo heard Professor Okpara calling it a day. To drive the message home, he said, 'People, it's tragic that it always takes something like this for us to get together as fellow Nigerians. The last time I saw most of you was when we went to mourn Mandela. I was glad to meet some of you for the first time then. Let us not make it a habit to meet only when something tragic happens . . .'

A murmur of assent.

'I think, as the young people have suggested, we need to strike while the iron is still hot. We march to the ANC head-quarters; we march to the Union Buildings. Behind the doors, meetings do not always elicit firm commitments from parties concerned. But if we march publicly, in the glare of the media and the international community, everyone will be under pressure to act. My friends, tomorrow is going to be a long day indeed. And the days ahead are going to be more challenging. Now, let's go and sleep.'

'How can we sleep when the beds are burning?' Mrs Okpara said, leading Nomcebo and the women who'd been sitting with her in the dining room back into the lounge.

'Darling,' said Professor Okpara, 'we need to preserve our strength. We have a few long days ahead.'

'Those Australian boys saw these things coming. A long time ago. How can we dance when the earth is turning? Yeah, we won't be sleeping properly for the next few days, weeks. How indeed can we sleep when the beds are burning?'

'What exactly are you saying?' her husband asked.

'We are staging a night vigil, right here, right now!'

Mrs Obaigbena had woken up. She said, 'Aha, you're sensible, after all. Even for a West Indian. We are staging a night vigil right here . . .'

Mrs Okpara continued, 'We are going to phone all the available late-night radio shows and express our outrage. Create a movement. Those of you who blog will blog. The young people will tweet and facebook and what have you! We will sing and dance and capture the activities on YouTube! Our enemies have used social media against us, but we'll reclaim it for ourselves.'

Someone started a religious song with a fast tempo. Suddenly the house exploded with the clapping of hands.

Mrs Okpara continued, 'We are going to act! We are going to make our voice heard. Occupy Wall Street did not give birth to itself; it was birthed by people who felt outraged, people who did not want to sit in the corner and cry, people who want to take their destinies into their own hands . . .'

'Say it, sister!'

'We are going to start a movement. We can't sleep. These

beds are burning. But we can dance, even if the earth is turning. For we are made of sterner stuff. We are going to sing, and write, shout, and blog, and dance until the walls of officialdom listen to us . . .'

'Tell the truth and shame the devil!'

'Like the people of Jericho, we are going to chant around the walls of Pretoria and Luthuli House until they collapse under the righteousness of our voices. We shall not be silenced. No, we're not going to sleep! These beds are burning. We are not going to burn and die in our sleep!'

Learning to Love

Six months since his arrival at Harvard and still no pussy. It riles Vusi that in a collection of steamy stories he's just finished reading, assholes with no class, no money, and no education are all getting laid in this very town of Cambridge, Boston. Yet he, with his two degrees, a beautiful apartment and some scratch in the bank, cannot seem to score. Where is the justice in this?

In South Africa, this was not the case. He had a woman for every day of the week. Ntombs slept at his place on Monday. On Tuesday it was Juanita's turn. Vuyokazi came on Wednesday. Lisa rocked up on Thursday. Then there was a yawning chasm between Friday and Sunday, when anything could happen. That was until Ntombs decided, as his main woman, to assert her authority and take Friday nights as well. She showed up at his flat one Friday with the key he gave her and found him having sex with a light-skinned woman he picked up at a bar. He thought she was going to kill the poor girl. 'Is this what you do behind my back, Vusi?' Ntombs had said, a huge steak knife from the kitchen in her hand. 'I know this whore is not Juanita, nor is she Vuyokazi, nor Lisa. At least I have an understanding with those three. They respect my position in this set-up. Not some yellow bitch I've never seen before. I'm going to kill her. Move out of the way so I can get to her. Whore! Woza la sfebe!' The other woman fled half-naked.

Nothing more was said on the matter, but Ntombs made sure she got her revenge. That Monday night he found her in bed, pretending to be reading a novel. Only, she was holding it upside down. As soon as he slid in under the covers, she pounced on him. She pawed him, clawed him, slapped him, rode him until the traffic noises in the street died. Afterwards, he fell asleep, but it was not long before she yanked at his manhood, startling him to wakefulness. He complained. He was still complaining when she impaled herself on his erect member. She rode him. Until the first taxis and buses started honking their horns, reminding all and sundry to get out of their beds and greet the new day.

When he got home later that day, Juanita was there, waiting in her sexiest red nightie. He groaned. The way she pulverised him in bed that night, it was clear she and Ntombs were in cahoots. It was clear the girls had made a pact: nail the bastard.

As always happens with these things, his reputation in the street soared. Women showered him with smiles wherever he went.

But now he is in America, all alone, taking tortuous walks down Harvard Yard. Tortuous because the place is always teaming with hos in all shapes and sizes. If you were to pause and inhale the air, you could catch the heady aroma of pussy on those grounds. In fact, that's all he does these days: take a casual, nonchalant walk on the Yard, and inhale as much pussy aroma as he can. Then rush off to the nearest convenient corner to take matters into his own hands. Needless to say, he always feels dirty after this. 'Is this really me, me, me, Vusi of a hundred and one girls? A Harvard man, a Master of the Universe in the making, but look at me conducting a one-armed struggle in a toilet!' The one-armed struggle. That's what they call it back home.

Back home, the brothers would have called an emergency meeting. They would have enlisted the services of a medicine man. 'Throw your holy bones, old man, let them speak. Let them tell us who has bewitched this young man that he's lost his ability to ask for what's between a woman's legs. Throw the bones, old man!'

There is no medicine man here at Harvard. No divine bones to do the talking. He's alone, all alone. It's not for lack of trying that he finds himself in these dry straits. He has tried. God knows he has. Back home in South Africa, people don't court as they do in Thomas Hardy novels, nor do they 'date' as they do in America. Instead, if a man encounters a woman in the street, is it not considered rude when he doesn't stop her, share some small talk with her, make complimentary remarks about her legs, her backside, her eyes? Surely a woman who does not get stopped begins to doubt her womanhood. She gets called umgodi onganukwanja – a hole that not even dogs sniff at. Like dogs, men are always sniffing around.

While the man is going on about her beautiful figure, the girl will say, 'This figure, these legs, this beautiful face, they all come at a price. How big is your collection of cattle?' This is called ukushela. The two of them know it's a game. Traditionally, a man would not even ask for her address. If they encountered each other again by chance, things would get serious. It was thought the gods wanted them to consummate the relationship. Vusi had heard that, in ancient times, young men would accost young lasses by the riverside, and start reciting stories of valour. 'Look at me, young princess – I am the one who killed the lion with his hands. I drink beer with crocodiles. I soar in the skies with the eagles. With me on your side, you will never starve.'

That was then. In contemporary times, the boys hang around shop fronts, making catcalls at passing girls. But the poetry persists, he believes: 'Yo, babes, when I see you, I wanna pull my piece and shoot a nigga. That's how bad my love is for you.'

'Yo, sweetiepie, Beyoncé tells me she wishes she were you. Don't you want me to be your Jay-Z?'

'I don't do the Chris Brown thing to women. I give them love, not punches. How about you give me your digits and we take it from there?'

Back home, Vusi was respected for his skill at this poetry thing. And he always scored.

With this solid reputation, Vusi thought he was going to have a field day in America. He had watched a number of romantic movies so he could know how to get inside an American woman's pants. According to those films: you meet a girl in class, give her the look, ask her for a date to the movies. Do it again the second time, except this time you don't take her to the movies, you take her to dinner. Do it the third time, except this time you take her to the movies, then dinner, then to a club for a drink or two. Then to bed. In all the movies he had seen, there had been no exchange of poetry between the man and woman, no verbal sparring. Which is why he thought America would be a walk in the park.

When Vusi felt he was ready, he took a leisurely walk down Harvard Yard until he saw what he was looking for. He had seen this girl a number of times at the canteen in the Science building; at Gretel's Den; at Raven Used Books. She was always by herself. On the number of occasions he'd encountered her, she'd always smiled at him, her green eyes glowing with warmth, her lips (painted pink) pouting seductively. She was the one. He had to make his move.

'Hey,' he said, 'isn't it a lovely day?'

She paused, looked at him, unsmiling. (This was not in the script.)

He persisted: 'How are you this afternoon?'

'Do I know you?' (Another rude deviation from the script.)

'Yeah, you and I have known each other for, like, wow, centuries now. Gretel's, Raven Used Books, Science building canteen, Sociology lecture hall.'

'Get to the point.'

'Without sounding presumptuous, or anything, I think my people were right when they said one has to cross rivers and oceans, and brave forests and jump borders in order to find the crown. And I think I've found my crown. I've found true love. I've found you. Now, are you going to open your lovely heart so I can enter and give you the true love you clearly are in need of?'

'Fucking creep!' She stormed away. A trio of women passing by laughed out loud.

According to Vusi's experience of sparring in South Africa, when a woman gives you this kind of attitude, she is merely encouraging you to pull up your socks, to look for new words, a new approach, a new script. Which is why Vusi conveniently bumped into the woman outside Gretel's Den again a few days later.

'Ah,' he beamed at her, 'my people were correct when they said one's feet do not have a nose. They never know where they'll one day lead one to. Look where my feet have taken me. They have taken me to Gretel's, where I have just bumped into my long-lost friend who wants to have a drink with me. Indulge me, my dear – let me buy you a drink. You know we're both sick. We need each other.'

'You again!' she said in a loud voice. 'I'm gonna call the police, I swear to God.' Some passers-by stopped to stare.

When Vusi got to his apartment, he sat drinking beer, re-playing the scene in his mind. It soon dawned on him that this was a dangerous woman. She was one of those solitary types who did not know how to speak to other human beings. Leave her alone.

His next target was a black woman, from Africa somewhere, judging by her intricate hairstyle. He had seen her twice be-fore. Always drinking coffee, her nose buried in a book. She responded warmly enough when he greeted her at the canteen. She didn't object when he asked if he could join her. They sat together drinking coffee, eating donuts. The Soccer World Cup was on, which gave him an excuse to start talking soccer to her. To his relief, she was interested. Fairly knowledgeable about the sport, she was a Real Madrid fan. He had to reinvent him-self as a lover of this club even though his first and only love was Manchester United, the Red Devils. After coffee, they got up. Before the opportunity slipped out of his hands, he pounced. But he decided to do things the American way this time: he asked her out on a date.

She looked long and hard at him. 'What's your name again, brother?'

'Ah, sorry, my bad. Should have introduced myself properly, name is Vusi.'

'Mine is Grace. Say, Vusi, where you from?'

'Africa.'

'Yeah, that I could tell. I am also from Africa. Kenya. But which part of the continent are you from?'

'Kenya! Great to meet you, child of Jomo Kenyatta!' He beamed, showing her he was hip to Kenyan history. 'I am from Johannesburg, South Africa.'

'Johannesburg,' she muttered.

'Yeah, Joburg, Jozi! The City of Gold!' he offered enthusiastically.

'In Johannesburg, do black men go out on a date with women? That's a white thing! You black South Africans are fucked up.' Unexpected rage seemed to well within her. 'Asking a woman out on a date. That's messed up, you know. Why don't you just state your case here and now? That's how we do it in real Africa. Not that messed-up, schizophrenic shithole of a country.'

'I was trying to do things the American way. I am Zulu through and through – I'll sing you some Zulu poetry right now, if you want.'

She turned around the corner, muttering, 'Confused South African whities in dark skins.'

That was three months ago.

He hasn't stopped trying. As far as he can remember, somewhere in the Bible it says something like 'knock, and the door shall be opened. Ask and you shall be given.' But it has since dawned on him that he needs to learn a new language in order to be able to ask properly when the door is finally opened. No use in knocking on the door and when they open, you are standing there with your mouth hanging open, your thumb up your ass. Learn a new language, son.

At this rate, he is no longer discriminating about the kind of ikuku he might settle for. It doesn't have to be a college girl. Even a factory girl will do. Do they have factories around here? Even a street cleaner will do. He doesn't care about colour any more. White, black, Latino, Oriental. The other day he tried to stop a Filipino woman. She smiled. And ran off. Really took off. Like Usain Bolt. Everyone stared, looking at the fleeing woman and glaring accusingly at him. Every now and then he pays for the services of a woman. But paid-for pussy can't match spoken-for pussy. Never.

His life is one untrammelled calamity. Whereas in the past he used to cook his own meals, now he eats like Americans: either orders pizza online or takes his chances with those abominable TV dinners. He's quit the gym. His toned body has degenerated into a shapeless sack. He has stopped running. He has what they call love handles, except there is no one to handle them. His pectorals have become sad moobs. Not even a middle-aged woman who's breastfed three children would own up to his kind of boobs. He stopped shaving a long time ago. He's become sensitive too. Takes to criticism the way gasoline does to a burning matchstick. When a classmate said something about his beard, he exploded, 'What my beard got to do with your fucking self? Leave my beard alone.'

He's even stopped working on his accent. Yes, the accent. When you arrive in America, you work on your accent. That is obligatory. Americans must be able to make sense of what you are saying. Speak in a manner they can relate to. Doesn't matter if you're from England or India, Africa or Asia. Work on your accent, baby. If you get interviewed on TV and speak English in your native accent? American producers will add subtitles. No compromise there.

Now, when Vusi gets drunk – which is often these days – his native accent gets up on its feet. His accent stands between him and whatever girl he is trying to chat up at the bar.

A friend has suggested he take up yoga. To get him to take it easy on the booze, get in touch with his sensitive self again. Cleanse the mind of problems. Because he has nothing to lose, he takes up yoga. A few weeks later, he is happy to realise that yoga has restored his natural shyness. People seem to like that. When he speaks in his soft tones, they lean forward to listen to whatever he is saying. It's good when a beautiful woman leans forward so close to his face he can smell her shampoo and her mouthwash too.

This yoga seems to be working. It inspires him to start lifting weights again. And start jogging. He gets so immersed in yoga, he even forgets the reason he took it up in the first place: to temper his anger and help him achieve a sense of humility that will allow him to learn the language of courting – the American way. Then, suddenly, his eyes open up. His yoga classmates snap into focus. He realises that the yoga class is awash with beautiful women. How could he have missed that? He is happy he is one of a few men in this class. The ratio is about six to one. The other guys don't count for much. They wear earrings and Lycra unitards. They are all gay. Or that's what he thinks, until he sees one of them kiss a woman deep in the mouth, and proceed to ask about, 'Sam and Gwen – you picked them up from school, or did your mom fetch them?' Clearly a married couple. Yes, he notices the wedding rings. But still, a married man in a unitard?

His further assessment of the women in class makes him realise – surprise, surprise – they are extremely thin. So thin you can almost see through them. 'Social X-rays', as Tom Wolfe called them. But, hey, he is not here looking for a wife. Someone to warm his bed, that's all. A thin woman can be a start. After all, Iraq was not demolished in one day. Look on the bright side, Vusi. There are women smiling at you for the first time in a long while. When they speak to you, they lean so far forward you can even smell their shampoo. That's a start.

Things are going well. One night his yoga instructor calls him aside when everyone is gone. When your yoga instructor calls you aside, it could be one of two things, Vusi assumes: she wants you to quit class because you bring negative vibes, a dark aura; or, she wants to give you the good stuff. Sex that will make you levitate. As he walks into the instructor's office, there are voices in his head: *Don't blow it now, don't. Don't venture into your African poetry. Smell that? That's pussy. You're being offered some. Don't blow it.*

She says, 'You've put a lot of work into the physical side of yoga. But now we need to work more on your spirituality, your aura. Here's a book you need to read.'

That's all she offers. A book. It's a big tome. He lugs it home. So heavy it makes him think of his five-kilogram dumbbells. It's a book on transcendental meditation by some Maharish Something. Goddammit, does a man have to go through this just to get fuckable again?

Three days later, he is back at yoga class. He is in his own space, greeting his classmates even though he cannot truly see them. He is in that space he used to occupy when he was smoking a lot of weed back home in South Africa. Except he hasn't smoked in a long time. He has acquired a new ability to be with people while he is not with them. To scale the Rockies, swim the Atlantic while conducting a conversation with a person at the same time. He dreams as he walks. He dreams as he lifts his weights. He dreams as the women at the yoga class converse with him, leaning forward so he can smell their shampoo. And their mouthwash too.

He is in one of his dream modes when he encounters a woman who looks vaguely familiar outside CVS Pharmacy.

'Hey,' she says cheerfully, 'brother from Africa, how I love your positive vibe and sense of humour!'

She knows me? He smiles back. 'Hey, how've you been?'

'I know you don't recognise me, what with my hoodie and all the layers of clothing on me. I look like a grizzly bear. I'm Norma.'

Still can't place her. But he takes his chances. 'I know you also don't know my name.' He pauses. And he is right – she's blushing. 'I am Vusi. It's a shortened form of Vusisizwe. You see, Vusisizwe means "the one who will revive the nation". You see, in Africa—'

An inner voice shouts, *Stop it, stop it, stop it now.*

He recovers: 'Ah, Norma, I'm getting carried away with this African shit, you know what I'm sayin'. The name is Vusi, yes, Vusi.'

'You know, I'm so embarrassed we've known each other

for so long yet I've never asked your name. Good to finally meet you, Vusi. Listen, Vusi, you mind holding on to this dog while I go inside?'

For the first time, he realises she is holding a dog by a leash. It's one of the nice, big fluffy dogs. Breed? Fuck if he knows. Where he comes from dogs are dogs. Where he comes from you have a big dog. You have a small dog. You have an average dog. You have a dog with shaggy fur. You have a dog with scabs and fleas and shit. You have a dog that growls. You have a dog that yips. But dogs that yip don't last long. They get eaten by dogs that growl. Only in books does he read of German shepherds, Rottweilers, huskies and whatevershit. Wouldn't recognise a Rhodesian ridgeback if it peed on his shoes.

Still, he smiles as he accepts the leash. The dog looks up at him with its bright, innocent eyes. Strange! He's so used to the dogs owned by white people back home having a nasty attitude towards black people. Black men in particular. They start barking the minute they see a black man. Sometimes even before they see him. The minute they get a whiff of his scent, they start barking. Then madam knows there's a darkie around the corner. But this dog here seems so friendly. If it could, it would be giving him the proper Boston liberal smile. It's wagging its tail now.

Norma is back. 'Isn't she lovely?'

'She's a winner.'

'Wow, your accent is so cute. I love those, whatchamacallit? African speech cadences. Speech patterns? I love it. Can you say it again?'

He merely laughs, throwing his head back.

'Listen to *that* boisterous laugh!'

She pats him on the shoulder. To a passer-by they are good buddies, or even lovers, walking a dog. Walking along the snow-covered pavement, in their beautiful, heavy coats, and earmuffs and gloves. Splendiferous.

'How are you liking the classes?'

What classes could she be referring to? He steals another glance at her. The penny drops: she is in his yoga class. She is the one who's always muttering to herself. The banking executive, or what have you. Unlike the others – the social X-rays – her body is fuller, curvaceous, if he recalls. But her habit of speaking to herself gives him the creeps.

'Oops,' he says, 'I better get goin', man. Books and shit, know what I'm sayin'.'

'Listen, Vusi. How about . . .'

Her mobile starts ringing. She picks up, speaks briefly, then rings off.

'As I was saying . . .'

'Yeah, I really have to go home.'

'You know, every time I see you in class, you have this . . . this haunted look in your eyes. You're hurting.'

He doesn't know how to respond.

She's looking at him meaningfully. 'I think we need to deal with this . . .'

He stares at her. The dog wags its tail. It makes a polite 'woof, woof'.

'We need to deal with this shit,' she says rapidly. 'I'm not offering you love or anything, but you know . . .'

'Yes?'

'Let's go fuck. My place. Can you handle that?'

Two years later, it is his graduation ceremony. He rushes home afterwards, bursts into the house. Norma is at the kitchen table. She's fallen asleep in front of a bowl of soup.

She is startled into wakefulness. 'Wow! Look who's back. The Master of Universe himself! Congratulations, honey.'

'Thank you. How's the baby?' He strides towards a corner, where a colourful cot sits. Smiling, he touches the tiny hand. 'Yo, champ, how're ya doin'? Your dad is a Master of the Universe, at last.'

He looks around the kitchen, says, 'Didn't you say you were going to start packing today? It's two weeks before we go! We're not going to New Haven or something. We're going to Africa, remember?'

'No, the baby kept me busy.'

He kisses her wedding ring, looks at the bowl of soup. 'You haven't eaten. You need to eat in order to produce milk.'

'You're making a pig of me!'

He looks at her with her hair in all directions, the robe with what seems like the baby's spittle all over her shoulder, and chooses not to say anything. Instead, he kisses her puffy face, massages her oversized breasts. He reheats the soup, brings it back to the table.

'Eat.' He spoons the soup into her mouth.

First spoon, second, third, fourth. Then she starts crying.

'Why're you crying?'

'You're making me look silly, feeding me soup like this.'

'Okay, here's the spoon – feed yourself.'

She bawls even harder, tears and snot dropping into the bowl. 'I didn't say you must stop. You're making me look and feel stupid! Look how puffy and fat I am.'

He gets up.

'I want more soup. Feed me, silly.'

At length, she blows her nose on a Kleenex, wipes her mouth. Then says, 'Now, do you really want your son's name to be Conqueror of Nations?'

'When you say it in English, it sounds daft. Say it in Zulu: Nqobizizwe. Short, simple, powerful.'

'Can't get those click sounds, dammit!'

'You taught me the language of true love. Now you gotta learn those African clicks. That too much to ask for?'

As if stung by a bee, she shoots to her feet. She draws herself to her full height, thrusts her chin forward. 'Now, I shall speak.'

He instinctively rears back, as if from a blow to his face. 'Yo, what's up, babes? What's eatin' you?'

'I said: I shall speak. Uninterrupted. You know what, Vusi, I don't know what's got into you . . .'

'But, babes—'

She spears his chest with her finger. 'I said, shut the fuck up while I speak! You're not the guy I met those many months ago; you're not the sensitive, caring man I married. I don't know what America's done to you, or how you've completely misread America, but hell, you've become a talkative, insensitive piece of shit, you know that?'

Arms extended, he tries to give her a reassuring embrace. 'Come on—'

'Don't touch me! Listen, I might be older than you and you might think I'm desperate for your love, desperate for your African dick that you're so in love with, well, I've got news for you, babe. I'm not naming my baby some Conqueror of Nations shit.'

'It's not your decision to make. I'm the father.'

'I don't know what America has done to your lovely mind, don't know how you've read America. But certainly the America that you carry in your head is not real. When I first met you, you were nice and polite. Now all of a sudden, you're cussing all over the place. Shit-that, pussy-that. You think that's America?'

'Wait, where is this tirade going?'

'Listen.' She sighs. 'I never thought I would fight with you like this. But I am not naming my baby Conqueror.'

'He's my baby too!'

'Number two, I am not going to Africa with you. I've cancelled the reservations.'

'What the . . .' He swallows the offending word before it comes out. 'But why have you done that?'

'I'll only accede to your request on one condition.'

'Yes?'

'You're going to take gender sensitivity classes.'

'Are you for real? Do those things really exist, or are they movie fodder?'

'With assholes like you around, we need them, and we've created them. But of course I can't force you. It should come from deep inside your heart, the preparedness to fix your shit.'

'Look who's cussing now!'

'See how it feels being cussed at.' She pauses. 'So, are you in?'

'Well,' he says, biting his lip, 'how long do these classes take?'

'Depends on you. Could be two months or six months. Just like rehab. The harder you work at fighting the habit, the better.'

'Do I really have to do that? I mean, I can mend my ways here at home, even as we travel to Africa.'

She stares at him with cold eyes. 'Are you in or are you out? This is not a joke.'

'Okay, where's this place anyway, and when can I start?'

'Here,' she says, handing him a brochure, 'the class has already been paid for. The sooner you start, the better.'

'Babes, can't we talk about this? Maybe you need to cancel the classes, please, babes.'

'First lesson, even before you get to that class: stop calling me FUCKING BABES. You hear that?'

'Sorry, b— darling. This is so unnecessary and embarrassing. Can we reconsider?'

She thrusts her palm into his face: 'Speak to the hand, brother. You need to learn a new language.'

TP Phiri, Esquire

'What do you want here?' The man glares at Shirley, blocking the door. She jerks her head to the side, grins in hopeful disbelief, as if to say: *Excuse me, can you say that again?*

In the manner of one striving to be patient with a dimwit, the man enunciates the same words, now in Zulu: 'Ufunani lapha?'

It has been drizzling all morning. A light, incessant drizzle, the kind of which can go on for an entire weekend. But as soon as Shirley entered the premises, and started driving up the driveway, it came down with unexpected vehemence. On any other day, she would certainly have enjoyed the trip up the cobbled driveway, bounded on either side by cucumber-green lawns and colourful flowerbeds. She would have paused to take it all in, because she was seeing it for the first time. But not today.

Although she is standing under a decent awning, stray raindrops can still reach her shoes.

'Man, are you going to let me in?' she says, irritation creeping into her voice now. 'I'm here to see Gershwin.'

'Is he expecting you?'

'This man!' She throws her hands in the air, paces up and down. 'Just who the hell do you think you are?'

She sizes him up. Black shoes polished to a blinding shine, black formal trousers with creases so sharp they could slice a fly into two pieces. An off-white shirt with expensive-looking cufflinks and, finally, a black bow tie. His head is clean-shaven. His face is pitch black, with a rich sheen. A handlebar moustache, speckled with grey, makes him look like a South African policeman from a bygone era.

'Theophilus P Phiri, Esquire. That's the name. Citizen of Blantyre, British Nyasaland. That's my heritage. Pity they renamed my country "Malawi". Thanks to that misguided Independence nonsense. Bring back the British Empire, I always say. So, what is your next question? You still haven't answered *my* question: is the master expecting you?'

From inside the house, a voice calls out: 'Theo, what's happening out there? Where's my drink?'

'Some strange lady has come to our door unannounced. Johannesburg is so full of wandering strangers, who stumble onto people's doorsteps unannounced. I don't know why Themba let her past the gate in the first place. I shall remember to discipline him accordingly.'

The shuffling sound of feet approaches the door and Shirley glimpses Gershwin. 'Holy cow,' he half-screams, 'it's Shirley. Let her in, Theo. Let her in.'

'We're slipping, aren't we, Master? Our standards are going down,' Theophilus P Phiri mutters as he allows Shirley into a cavernous entrance hall.

'Sorry, Theo,' Gershwin says. 'I did leave her name with Themba at the gate when you were not around. I assumed he would have shared the information with you.'

'No, sir, I wasn't notified.'

'My bad, Theo, my bad.'

'Your meaning is obscure, sir. What is bad?'

'Ag, never mind.'

Gershwin is looking comfortable in his cream linen slacks, black moccasins, and black Polo golf shirt. Shirley throws herself into his welcoming arms. He gives her a kiss on the lips and they hug each other for a very long time. Theo is watching, waiting, a disapproving scowl on his face. Shirley ignores him. When they finally let each other go, Shirley points at the man observing them and says, 'Gersh, are you going to tell me what's going on here? Who is he?'

Gershwin laughs nervously. 'Has he been giving you a hard time, old Theo?'

Shirley puts her hands on her hips. 'I've never seen such a despicable display of bad manners.' She eyes Theophilus where he is standing to attention beside the closed door, his eyes now averted from them as if he cannot hear a word of their conversation.

'He can be a bit brusque, I know,' Gershwin says. 'But he's only doing his job. Darkies have no respect for one's private space. They drop in on you, unannounced, bringing the whole ghetto with them. And then proceed to demolish your entire cellar. You know what I'm saying is true.'

'Spoken like the snob you've always been. Are you going to offer me a drink or something? I'd get it myself but I don't know where the fridge is, seeing as you haven't bothered to invite me over to your new home since you've moved in here,' she says with playful reproach. 'What are you hiding anyway? A new girl in your life?'

Gershwin ignores her prying. 'Theo, I'm dying of thirst.'

The man's eyes snap to Gershwin. 'Will a Lagavulin do, or is it still too early, sir?'

'Seeing as I have a guest, bring us a trolley we can choose from.'

'Yes, sir.' Theophilus P Phiri turns on his heel and walks off.

Gershwin directs Shirley to the lounge, while he launches into an animated speech. 'He's the best manservant money can buy. Stubborn as a mule. But always fair. Always selfless in his pursuit of order in this house.'

'Manservant,' Shirley says, curling her lips in disgust, 'sounds so British. In South Africa, male servants cut the lawn, wash one's cars, change globes, fix cupboards. Sometimes help the wife out of her panties. In short, they do all the things that most men refuse to do at their homes. But they don't hover around the kitchen.'

They sit down on the expensive leather couches in the lounge. 'You're misreading the situation,' Gershwin says. 'I've got Themba who doubles as a security guard and a handyman, and then I have Sipho who takes care of the garden . . .'

'And what's his job?' Shirley inclines her head in the direction in which the man has disappeared.

'He runs the household. Sipho and Themba take instructions from him. And so does Mam'Sithole. That's the lady who comes in twice a week to do my laundry. So, Theo is my ears and eyes in this house. But can he cook!'

Shirley bursts out laughing. 'You allow a man to cook for you! Is that what money does to black men in South Africa these days? A man cooks for you?' She claps her hands the way rural women would to express surprise and disgust.

Unperturbed by her derision, Gershwin presses on: 'A friend of mine who runs a restaurant – you know the Pepe chain of restaurants? – yeah, the man who owns the entire chain has tried to steal Theo from me.'

Shirley hasn't stopped laughing. 'A man is cooking for you, in your own house! What kind of African man are you?'

Theo comes in pushing a trolley with an assortment of drinks. Lagavulin, Caol Ila, Johnnie Walker Black, Tanqueray, some red wines, and white ones too in an ice bucket.

He pours them their drinks – Lagavulin for Gersh and red wine for Shirley. She accepts her drink without a word.

'Theo, old man, there's a nasty revolution brewing in my stomach. Will you help douse the flames of protest in there? Something quick and fast, seeing as I don't want to detain Shirley for the whole day here. Young ladies like her have busy schedules.'

'TP Phiri to the rescue, sir.'

Gershwin gets up and pulls Shirley to her feet. He wraps his arm around her waist. 'Let me show you the rest of the house. You should see the view from the upstairs bedrooms. There are five of them.'

As they ascend the stairs, Shirley spots Theophilus from the corner of her eye. He is poking his head out of a door, staring up at them. She pretends not to see him shaking his head. What a strange man! She'll have to have a serious talk with Gershwin about his choice of staff. After an extensive tour of the enormous premises, they are sitting at the table in the dining room. Shirley and Gershwin are paying their undivided attention to the culinary magic Theo has managed to conjure at such short notice.

'You've outdone yourself once again, Theo,' Gershwin is gushing. 'These cutlets. They are ... what's the word you use for food when it tastes good?'

'Delicious?'

'Better than delicious. Also starts with a "d".'

'Oh, that would be divine, sir.'

'That's the one. Except they are the superlative of divine.'

'Not at all, sir. It was a contented lamb that offered its life for sir's absolute enjoyment.'

Shirley is chewing away, eyes closed, head thrown back in ecstasy.

'Shirley.' When Gersh says her name, her eyes fly open and she looks around her in embarrassment. Gersh has an irritatingly knowing smile on his face. 'How's your salmon? You seemed to be enjoying it.'

Refusing to offer any praise herself, she simply cuts a slice of the fish and reaches across the table, delivering the morsel to Gersh's expectant mouth. He chews for a few moments. Then he says, 'Ah, Theo, I can picture you chartering a Concorde to have this salmon delivered here, straight from Scotland!'

An hour later, Gershwin and Shirley are back in the lounge on the biggest couch. Gershwin asked Theo to bring them a blanket, which he did with a sour expression, and now they have draped it over both of them. In the rainy weather, they are snuggling under the blanket, sipping red wine.

She gives lip: 'How did you land your hands on this . . . this manservant of yours?'

'The man knows the way to an angry lady's heart is through her stomach. I can see you are even smiling now. He's good, isn't he?'

'You haven't answered my question,' Shirley says, pursing her lips to hide her smile.

'Ag, it's a long story, Shirley.'

'I'm waiting. Patiently.'

'He's a Malawian chap. I know your dislike for foreigners is legendary . . .'

Shirley puts her drink down on a side table and looks Gersh in the eye. 'It can be dangerous, what you're doing. They're killing kwerekweres these days. You don't want to be caught in the crossfire. Is he even documented?'

'Don't be like that. It's the troublesome foreigners they are after. The drug dealers, the human traffickers, the fraudsters . . .'

'You still haven't answered my question: how did you get to recruit him?'

Gershwin sighs. 'About three months ago, he came around and sweet-talked my housemaid into opening the gate for him.'

'Just like that?' Shirley throws her hands in the air. 'I know you're a careless man, but I didn't realise you were irresponsible as well. What if he were an armed robber? Not for nothing do Johannesburgers put up walls around their houses. This city is dangerous.'

'Okay, let me put it in proper context.' He puts his glass down as well, as if he were afraid she might accidentally knock it out of his hands. 'The maid spoke to him on the intercom. But the man prevailed on her to hand the intercom receiver to me. Which she did.'

'And you buzzed him in?' She rolls her eyes.

'Are you going to listen?'

'Sorry.'

'The man caught me off-guard. He was so smooth, his English exquisite and quaint, and his sense of humour irresistible. So I buzzed him in.' He holds up a hand to stop her from interrupting again. 'And now, listen to this: when he walked in, he looked like some Hollywood type from the fifties in his off-white three-piece suit and matching fedora. He didn't waste time. Got right down to business, standing right there at the door. Said a guy, Steve Chirwali, had referred him to me. The name sounded familiar and, as he described the guy, it soon turned out that the man used to be close to my dad. They used to play horses together. The man is a Malawian guy himself. And my father used to love Malawian women, you might have heard. Back in the days of apartheid. Those days we never imagined there'd come a time when we would hate other black people simply based on their country of origin. Apartheid kept us together as black people, whether we were Malawian, Nigerian, Zambian or whatever. But once we defeated that monster, we created our own monster: xenophobia. Isn't that funny?'

Shirley sighs dramatically. 'I abhor political speeches.'

'Anyway, when my mother wasn't looking, my father used to chase Malawian women—'

'And my mother warned him against the bloody Malawians. Told him they would ruin him.'

'Your mother was young, naïve, jealous. She thought she was protecting her brother. But she didn't quite understand my father.'

'My mother saw this a long time ago: you can't trust these foreigners. They must go back to their bloody countries, bloody leeches. She must have seen what those women did to your father.'

Gershwin wags a finger at her. 'Young lady, I'm the one who's telling the story. Anyway, having listened to what Theo had to say, I dismissed him. A few hours later, I got in touch with Steve, the man who'd referred him. He confirmed the applicant's story. And gave me more dope on him. Said he had a clean record, was hard-working and, like all Malawians, super reliable. But what my contact found intriguing was that this man had turned down other job offers. He said he wanted to work for me, Mr Jacob Cele's son.'

'Nothing wrong with that, per se.' Shirley shrugs. 'Your father was rich and famous. And so are you. You're always in the papers.'

'Right. But me being me, I put it down to the power of prayer. You know me and my faith. I thought this forthright man would protect me from all the gold diggers of the world. Chance takers who've darkened my door and proceeded to soil my sheets over the past few years . . .'

'And left you heart broken, and your house almost bare.'

'You don't have to rub it in, but you're right.' Gersh picks up his wine and takes a sip. 'I don't know why it's always the good guys who get kicked in the teeth by you ladies. Anyway, I took him on. First week on the job, he got me to hire a security guard who'd live on the premises. He enlisted the services of a gardener. He retained Mam'Sithole, the lady who cleans the house and does my laundry. That's efficiency in anyone's book.'

'Has his cooking always been this good? Or was this just a fluke.' She is loath to admit that she enjoyed every bite of the meal, especially now that she knows the cook is a Malawian whom Gershwin has employed off the street, so to speak. 'Doesn't take much skill to grill salmon and lamb cutlets anyway.'

'The green-eyed monster!' Gersh laughs. 'Give credit where it's due. The man's good. In fact, I must enter him into one of these Best Chef competitions on TV. He'll show his competitors the eye of a worm, as our people say.'

'But you still must be careful. Con artists are like that. Not for nothing are they called that. They prey on one's confidence. And when one's guard is down: bang! They pounce.'

'I'm not a fool, Shirley. All those women who've stolen from me have taught me a lesson.' He leans forward, lowers his voice to a whisper. 'I've got a private detective who gives me regular reports on him: who his friends are, where he hangs out when is off-duty, that kind of stuff. My dick guy has always given him a clean bill of health.'

She grunts, shrugs. He sips his drink, sits back in his chair, and declares, 'With him around, I'm like a king in his castle. But . . .' He hesitates, lowers his voice again. 'My hidden camera caught him on three occasions rummaging through my documents. For a moment there, I thought he'd been sent by a competitor to fish for intelligence. You know, there is a real danger of that, when you're an IT manager at a company as big as mine. But, no. All he was interested in were my family albums, such as they are. He spent a considerable amount of time going through them. But, as you know, I don't have much in the way of family pictures. Some from my first wedding. Some of me as a young man. Me and friends, girlfriends. Old family photos from when we were little. There's the cutest one of me and you: I'm five and you're about two. It was taken shortly after you and your mother came to stay with us, after your father disappeared.'

'Let's not go there. Please!'

'Okay, I didn't mean to talk about your father.' He is silent for a moment. 'But . . . it *has* always intrigued me that you insist on using the asshole's surname and yet you hate him so much.'

'I said, move on!'

'Anyway . . . where was I? Ah, Phiri rummaging through my drawers. I have that footage of him spending a lot of time going through family albums, reading some of my letters, such as they are. At the suggestion of my private detective, I deliberately left my safe unlocked one day, thinking he would steal my jewellery. We thought the time had come to nail him. But no, he wasn't interested.'

'You sure he didn't take your ID and passport and get them copied?' Shirley narrows her eyes. 'That's how these bloody foreigners make their living: stealing people's identities and selling them to the highest bidder.'

'He did look at my passport and my ID,' Gershwin admits. 'But he never removed them from my bedroom. Nor did he appear to be copying my ID number. I scrutinised the footage endlessly, just double-checking that aspect of things.'

'Ha! These foreigners have minds that work like a computer. They have photographic memories. Maybe he's already sold your ID number to someone.'

Gershwin waves her comment away. 'His encounter with pans and pots always produces something that inspires the palate. The added bonus: he's also a fount of wisdom. About women, African politics, horse racing . . .'

'See? Typical conman.'

'No, man. He's my Jeeves.'

'What's a "Jeeves"?'

Gershwin, who has just taken a sip of wine, splutters and jumps out of his seat, spilling his drink in the process. He's succumbed to paroxysms of mirth.

'What's so funny?'

'"What is a Jeeves?" she says. My dear, it should be: *Who is Jeeves?*'

'Okay, suit yourself then. Who is Jeeves?'

'You studied at Sussex and you don't know one of the most celebrated characters in modern English literature? Hang your head in shame.'

'I'm an economist. Fiction is not my cup of tea.' Shirley crosses her arms and glares at him.

'Economists are the finest peddlers of fiction,' he retorts.

'We deal in facts and figures.'

'How wrong you are. You are into speculations, suppositions, projections. What if, what if? That's the question that drives your industry. What if? And that's the province of fiction.'

'Let's not change the subject. You still need to explain to me, why do you allow a mere foreigner to be rude to your guests?'

On her next visit to Gershwin's house, Shirley brings her beau, Mojalefa, along. After a sumptuous dinner, the men retire to the drawing room for cigars and cognac. She takes an unhurried walk to the kitchen.

'So, you're back,' Theo says without removing his eyes from the bowl of ice cream in his hands. His voice is cold. 'And this time you're with a man. My master was beginning to warm up to you, thinking he stood a chance with you. And what do you do? You bring your man with you. You're no different from the others who take advantage of Master's generosity and kindness.'

She gapes at him. 'What the fuck?'

His head jerks back, his eyes wide. It is clear a woman has never uttered such profanity in his presence.

'This shit must come to an end,' Shirley says. 'My cousin must fire you—'

'Your cousin! My master is your cousin?' The bowl slips out of his hands, crashes on the floor.

They look at each other, aghast. He's the first to recover. 'My apologies. Satan has taken possession of my hands. I'm breaking my master's plates for no reason at all, at all. Don't ever mention this encounter to my master, my dear madam. Prease.' She notices that, in his agitation, he mixes up his Rs and Ls. 'Prease, madam. Theo begs flom the bottom of his heart. God bress.' He pauses, looks at her again. 'Cousins? I saw you getting cosy with him the other day. Then I jumped to concrusions. God in heaven, he's your cousin!' He shakes his head as a boxer who's just been stung with a sledgehammer punch to the temple would. As if something has just dawned on him, he narrows his eyes and takes a close look at Shirley.

Startled, she rushes out of the kitchen, all the way to the drawing room where the men are smoking.

A month later, Shirley is sitting at her house, doing final preparations for a party she wants to throw on Freedom Day. It is at times like these that she misses having a mother. Hers died when she was only ten years old. Were her mother alive today, Shirley would have roped her into the planning, would have asked her advice on the finer details of entertaining. Mojalefa is a great boyfriend, but they haven't been together for long and he knows more about sports than dinner parties. She is sad to confess to herself that she can't think of anyone but Gershwin to help her with the final touches.

She gets into her car, drives over to his house. At the door, a smiling Theo welcomes her in. His transformation is amazing. His smile is from ear to ear. What has happened? 'Welcome home, Madam Shirley. Feel at home.' He ushers her straight in to the lounge. 'What shall I offer Madam, in the way of beverages?'

Shirley frowns in consternation.

Then Gershwin saunters into the lounge.

'Whassup, cuz? Something to drink? Oh, Theo has already sorted you out! Told you he is a professional.' Gershwin pecks Shirley on the lips, sinks into a sofa. 'Theo, what about me? A man can't start a day on a dry stomach.'

Theo brings him a beer.

'It's nice and sunny outside. Let's go sit by the pool.'

Theo leads the way, with his trolley of delicious drinks.

'A little bird tells me you are hosting the party of the year,' Gershwin says as he takes a seat in a wicker chair. 'But you still haven't invited your dearly beloved cousin. How's that?'

'Hold your horses, Gersh. That's exactly why I'm here.' Shirley sits down across from him. 'I've got everything worked out: people have RSVPed; enough booze. But there's a problem.'

'Fire away. No time to waste.'

Theo has parked his trolley next to them and Shirley sees him walk off to go speak to the gardener, who is pruning some shrubs on the other side of the pool.

She takes a deep breath. 'Ordinarily, I would have hired one of the catering ladies who always come to my rescue when I'm hosting a big crowd. But I think we need a change of pace. The stuff from the catering companies I've used has become so predictable, so blasé. I want something fresh, something new, something that will knock the socks off my friends' feet. Mind you, these parties are not just parties for the sake of being parties. There's a lot of networking that takes place there. Business, cuz, business.'

'So what do you propose to do?'

'Okay, I'll be blunt: may I enlist the services of your Malawian Jeeves?'

Gershwin laughs. 'You've finally discovered old Wodehouse. Reading is good. Even for nose-in-the-air economists.'

'So what do you think?'

'Frankly, I don't think Theo would want to do it. After all, you two hate each other's guts. And you know it.'

'You can prevail on him. Just for the party.'

He looks sideways, leans forward and whispers, 'You won't believe the nasty things he's been saying about you. Says you can't be my cousin. Says you want to steal from me. Says it with such conviction that I find myself shivering. Which is ridiculous, of course.'

She is looking at him straight in the eye, her mouth agape. A shadow falls over her. Theo smiles into her face. 'Another drink for Madam?' He refills her glass, pours a beer for Gershwin.

'Now that I have both of you together, may you indulge me a moment?'

Gershwin and Shirley look at each other, shrugging. Gershwin says, 'Proceed.'

'In the circles I move in, word is Madam here is hosting the party of the year on Freedom Day. A little bird further tells me Madam here has enlisted the services of a big-name chef from out of town. Now, as a self-taught upstart of a cook, poor Theo is thinking: *What if I ask Master for a day off?* I would love to visit Madam's abode, and meet the great chef himself. Poor

Theo won't cause any disturbance. He will observe from the sides. I learn by observing. The chef competitions on TV have left an impression on me. They've taught me lessons to last me a lifetime. Imagine, then, me rubbing shoulders with those big-name chefs. In the flesh, in the flesh! There, my humble request. My dear master, my dear madam.'

He leaves them looking at each other. Some louries are making a racket in a tree nearby.

She's the first to recover. 'Theo, please come back.'

There's a spring in his step as Theo approaches. He bows before her. 'Yes, Madam?'

'Theo, you are the chef everyone is talking about.'

'I don't understand, Madam.'

'You're the one who's going to be cooking for me. Name your price.'

Gershwin shoots up from his seat. 'Okay, a man must draw the line. Whatever game you're trying to play, Shirley, won't succeed. If you take him, it will only be for the party, cuz. Only for the party. Theo still belongs to this household; he's still the master of this residence.'

'I'm a man of the Empire, sir,' Theo jumps in. 'My un-divided loyalty is still with you. But it would indeed be an honour to be the humble recipient of Madam's generosity.'

'All right, then, all right.'

'Thank you, sir, I always knew my association with you would lead me to great things. To my destiny.'

After the party, everyone who's anyone of Johannesburg high society can't stop talking about it. There are tweets, Facebook comments, blog entries, pictures on Instagram and Tumblr. By all accounts, the party rocked. It was, everyone is saying, a fashion parade-music festival-gourmet food show all rolled into one. Snippets of the party appeared on *Top Billing*. The presenter signed off by posing the question: 'Has anyone ever heard of Chef TP Phiri, Esquire? He did a splendid job at Ms Shirley Mkhize's and now – *poof!* – he's disappeared into thin air. Who, exactly, is he? How come no one has ever heard of him? Where has he gone to? If you see him, tell him there's a slot for him on *Top Billing*.'

That's the question Shirley and Gershwin are asking themselves. Through their tears, they are watching, for the umpteenth time, a recorded version of the *Top Billing* episode. On the coffee table in front of them: two whisky glasses. Next to the glasses is a black-and-white picture they discovered in Shirley's bedroom after Theo had disappeared from her party. It had been lying next to photo albums taken from Shirley's bookshelf. But this was not one of Shirley's photos. Neither she nor Gershwin had ever seen it before that night. In the picture: a younger version of TP Phiri, Esquire, beaming into the camera. He has his left arm wrapped around a younger version of Shirley's mother, Nomthandazo.

In the picture, Nomthandazo – smiling as broadly as her man – is carrying a small bundle of life.

Ramu the Hermit

Ramu sat cross-legged in a meditative posture, his head held high and his eyes glued to the heavily curtained window. For a moment, his mind's eye rejoiced in the sight of a battalion of bejewelled Hindu deities, their foreheads resplendent with sacred ash and their bangles tinkling with every move they made. He saw a serpent, the holy serpent of Lord Shiva. It stood on its tail and swayed sideways to the music of the tablas and tambourines. The all-seeing Lord Krishna with his multiple hands sat serenely atop a chariot.

Suddenly Ramu's thread of communication with his gods was cut short, disturbed by the high-pitched voice of the muezzin calling from the mosque opposite his house. The impudence of these Muslims! Couldn't they conduct their prayers in silence, like everyone else?

While still muttering to himself, he could discern, in wavy ripples of sound, up-tempo music drifting from the house next door into his room of prayer. He cursed the earth and asked God why he tolerated the existence of such noisy people who disturbed him in prayer; people who didn't have any sense of decency; people who didn't have respect for the gods of others; people who were forever invading his privacy and making it impossible for him to communicate with his gods.

In his mind he tried to reconstruct the Divine Lord and his entourage, to no avail. Voices from the mosque rose and fell; the music from next door gained momentum. It was Friday, after all, a time when mere mortals like the people next door were beginning their orgy of noise, drunkenness and – oh, how could he allow his mind to be contaminated by the mere thought of the woman next door and her stream of male visitors?

He had chosen his way. The holy way. The only way to heaven. The gate to eternal happiness. He would not be moved.

'To hell with the devil,' Ramu muttered under his breath and tried to marshal his thoughts away from the filth surrounding him. Not for the first time, he made a mental note to start looking for better lodgings elsewhere, in a quieter, more civilised neighbourhood. He wished Kali, the goddess of death, could at that very instant come and wipe out all the sluts like the woman next door, bitches who had reduced their bodies – God's temples – into mere mattresses for all men to loll on indiscriminately for a price. Their bodies were now waste bins in which every man emptied his tank of unwanted garbage. He had read of the wrath of Kali. He shuddered when the goddess's sword took shape in his mind.

The number of bitches is definitely on the increase, he mused.

Why was he allowing his mind to flirt with such earthly, if not evil, thoughts? Was he not on the threshold of being a sanyasi, an ascetic whose life is devoted to the worship of the All-Wise, the Almighty?

His swami had taught him to chant the holy mantra in order to purge his mind of dirty thoughts. He started intoning: 'Hare Krishna, Hare Krishna, Krishna Krishna, Hare Hare, Hare Rama, Rama Rama, Hare Hare . . .'

He chanted for what seemed like hours, but as soon as he paused, worldly thoughts assailed his mind. How proud he was that he would be the first black African sanyasi in the whole of Chatsworth township. Well, of course there weren't many Africans – or blacks – in the township to begin with. The country's apartheid and segregation laws, which declared Chatsworth a residential area for people of Indian extraction, made sure of that. And the Africans who did live here were descendants of Zanzibaris who had been brought to Durban at the turn of the nineteenth century to work in white people's sugarcane plantations because the locals, proud and pig-headed as they were, had refused to work for foreigners in their own native land. Except for their skin colour, the new arrivals had nothing in common with the local blacks. They spoke Zanzibari or Swahili, while the local blacks spoke Zulu, Xhosa, Sotho and other indigenous southern African tongues. The Zanzibaris were of the Muslim faith, while local blacks generally subscribed to the Christian faith.

As a Zanzibari, Ramu too had been brought up under strict Muslim conditions. But now that he was twenty-four, he thought he was old enough to make his own decisions about the path he wanted to take. So, he had not so long ago 'defected', as his detractors said, to the Hare Krishna. He was lucky he was in South Africa. He knew that in such Muslim countries as Saudi Arabia the punishment for apostasy was death.

'Inshallah,' the cry strayed from the mosque, startling Ramu back to reality. The music continued to play at the house next door, more vigorously now.

I should have gone to the temple where there is no noise, Ramu thought. But again, his swami had insisted he keep away from the temple these days. He should stay indoors by himself so that he could learn self-discipline, restraint. His tenacity was on test. Gone were the days where he had to rely on his fellow worshippers for moral support and spiritual succour. He was on his own now.

Was he failing the test? What else could he do to rechannel his thoughts to the Almighty?

Impulsively, he paged through the *Bhagavad Gita* which had been resting in front of him. He scanned it carelessly and closed it again. He put it in front of him and broke into a shastra, a Vedic hymn, in yet another attempt to chase evil thoughts away from his room of prayer.

Within an instant, he became so absorbed in the hymn that he did not feel the numbness of his buttocks resulting from his hours of sitting in the otherwise uncomfortable lotus position on the bare floor. With his mind's eye, he saw himself in the midst of devotees in saffron robes dancing gaily as they crashed their cymbals. Others were beating their hand drums and singing their hearts out in praise of Lord Krishna.

He was so meditative he could feel his blood curdle with the ecstasy of spiritual rediscovery.

And then, as if in a dream, he heard a crackling sound echoing in his ears. Slowly and reluctantly, he emerged from his trance. He realised that he wasn't dreaming after all; there were screams and a jangle of *rat-a-tat* sounds outside. He jumped to his feet and peeped through his thick curtains.

But he couldn't see anything out there in the street. Cursing, he thought he might have been in holy dreamland. He closed the curtain and went to the picture of Lord Krishna that was hanging from a wall, and gave a slight bow before resuming his position on the floor. He tried to reconstruct his link with the spiritual world again. No sooner had he started chanting the mantra than he was jolted back to reality by the crash of his window and a missile missing him by inches. Evil spirits! Alarmed, he looked at the missile – a stone – that had fallen in a corner. It lay near his small table that was nearly invisible under the volumes of Sanskrit literature.

Nervously, he parted the curtains and peeped into the street, now enveloped in smoke and sound. Ah, he had smelt this before. Teargas! What was happening? Fiddling with his dhoti and slipping his feet into his sandals, he dashed for the door.

Once in the street, he saw it all: youths, each with his face masked with a towel, were stoning an armoured police vehicle. The police, some of them on top of the vehicle and others scattered all over the street, were systematically shooting at fleeing people. Why? Why on this street?

'Run, comrade! Don't let them catch you! Run!' a young man was shouting.

'Give them some guava juice, my bra! Throw the thing, throw the thing!'

A Molotov cocktail landed on the bonnet of the police vehicle. The car exploded in flames.

'The swine got me in the thigh!' someone cried.

Police guns continued to belch fire.

The praying and singing had long stopped at the mosque. So had the music at Ramu's neighbour's. People were running helter-skelter in the streets. The air was heavy with screams and the incessant bark of police guns.

Still dazed, Ramu felt something sting him on his bare left shoulder. Grimacing from the pain, Ramu dashed for safety.

His dhoti billowed as he fled. He jumped over the fence into a yard at the back of his house. There he crouched near a bush of tall dahlias. He recognised them by their smell, which he hated. Having seen another police vehicle driving slowly up the street he'd been running to, he decided to stay put among the malodorous dahlias. It would be unsafe to go and lock himself up in his house. The police were unpredictable during such times. They did not hesitate on mounting house-to-house raids, picking up any male they came across. They were ruthless. The State of Emergency gave them powers to arrest people without a warrant and detain them indefinitely, without charging them. They didn't give a rat's ass if you were a holy man.

Panting and dazed from the effects of the teargas, he touched the spot where the stray rubber bullet had caught him. The pain burnt and seemed to pierce the depths of his being. He was not bleeding profusely, but he felt as if the pain could kill him. Never in his life had he felt so much searing distress from such a small wound. Now he felt dizzy, weak. Rubber bullet wounds could be fatal sometimes, he'd been told.

The hullabaloo in the street had not subsided; the police vehicles were now racing up and down in pursuit of stone-throwing youths. The sound of the engines of the police vehicles was accompanied by the staccato sound of shooting. There were cries of agony. There were also expletives flying in the air.

He must have fallen unconscious for, when he next came to his senses, he was in a strange place. Flicking his eyes open nervously, he looked around. Ha! He was in a strange bed.

Fear gripped him, squeezing his heart. What had happened? Why was he here? He tried to prop himself up in the bed but he was too weak. Somebody appeared in the doorway. He squinted, allowing his eyes to absorb the figure. It was his neighbour, the woman who was every man's pillow. Rage welled in his heart. What would people say? He tried to sit up again, but fell back onto the bed. The woman smiled at him. She was carrying a tray bearing an orange, a banana and a glass of Coke.

Putting the tray on a dressing table, she loomed in the door-way, smiling. She leapt forward when she realised he was trying to get up.

'No, don't do that. You're hurting yourself. You're too weak, sir. I think you bled quite a bit. But I couldn't take you to the clinic. That would have been the end of you. The police were waiting at the entrance for people with gunshot wounds.'

'Weak? Who's weak? What am I doing here anyway?' He struggled to get up, but his body wouldn't carry him.

'Look at what time it is now. It's way past midnight. Have some fruit and go to sleep. You should rest. I'll explain every-thing to you in the morning.'

'No . . . you . . . you . . . tell me now what happened. Now, you witch! You sorceress. You slut. Have you bewitched me into coming into your bed like the rest of your men? Men who waste their holy seed on you?'

She merely smiled and smoothed the duvet over him. He realised with shock that he was naked. And he smelt of a strange perfume.

'What have you done to me? How did I get here? Tell me before I set the wrath of my God on you,' he said, pointing a finger at her.

'Okay,' she said, 'let me explain before you get too angry with me. I was running away from the police when I stumbled on you. You were lying unconscious near a bush. There was blood on your shoulder and on your clothes.'

He groaned.

'As soon as I recognised your face, I said to myself, "I can't let the holy man die out here in the wilderness." I decided to hide myself until the police had gone away so that I could take you home and nurse your wound.'

'You stinking daughter of the devil!'

'Wait, let me explain. I haven't done anything wrong. As a former nurse, I know how to treat severe bruises and wounds. I also know that inhaling teargas can complicate some people's respiratory system. So I was merely helping you.'

He concentrated hard on her, praying his intense gaze would make her disappear.

'As soon as the police vacated the area, I dragged you into the house so I could help you. I didn't realise such a thin man could be so heavy!' She laughed. He didn't.

The wall clock in an adjoining room chimed one o'clock.

She smiled. Her gown had slid open, and for the first time he noticed that she wore a transparent nightie that showed the better part of her thighs. At the joining of her thighs was a dark mound.

She was watching his eyes. She said, 'I think it's time for both of us to sleep. It's late. I'm dog tired.'

As an afterthought, she added, 'But first, have some cold drink and fruit.'

She roamed around the foot of the bed near the oak dressing table, which was laden with perfume bottles, an array of cream containers, combs of all shapes and sizes, and the unmentionable paraphernalia of her class, style, taste, trade.

'By the way,' she said in a voice that was now as smooth as the texture of her nightie, 'what's your name? Everyone calls you the holy man. But I'd like to know your name, darling.'

Ramu's temples were pounding steadily now. What would his swami say should he find him in the company of a woman notorious for her loose morals – a self-confessed, self-advertising, self-praising prostitute? One day standing in his yard, he'd heard her shouting in a drunken voice, telling a group of male visitors about her bedroom prowess. Now he was in her bed. What was the all-seeing Lord Krishna saying at this very moment? How had he allowed himself to be dragged into this lair?

His throat was suddenly parched. But he refused to drink the cold drink she had bought. He looked at her fixedly. Her stomach was a large blob of fat and her arms were as fleshy as huge bananas. Her big breasts heaved rhythmically when she laughed – which she did a lot. Her buttocks danced like jelly when she moved.

He asked himself what pleasure men derived from such an obnoxious-looking creature. He wanted to know why so many men paid their hard-earned money to loll on those rubbery arms. He couldn't understand why men risked breaking their marriages just because of this slut who belonged to the eternal inferno of hell.

His train of thought was brought to a standstill by the woman when she switched off the main light and slid into the warmth of the duvet cover beside him. 'What are you doing, what are you doing, slut?' He shifted towards the wall, avoiding the slightest contact with her.

Unperturbed, she slid closer to him. The bed was too small to allow space between them anyway. They had to huddle together. Or one of them had to sleep on the floor. Or perhaps there was a sofa in the living room he could use as a bed. He considered that. He tried to get up, but fell back onto the pillow. Neither of them uttered a word. The bedside lamp burned dimly, lending a touch of romance to this rather tense atmosphere. Still shifting uneasily, she paged through an old copy of a girlie magazine. He couldn't help catching a glimpse of a naked woman posing in positions he'd never imagined possible.

'As you do not wish to eat, let us sleep,' she said, sighing. She put the magazine on the bedside table and sank into the warmth of the bed.

Ramu's anger had transformed itself into inexplicable helplessness. His coldness had been thawed by the warmth of the human mass next to him. He was sweating again. His lips quivered, but words refused him. He could feel the blood coursing through every vein in his body. Now and then his body trembled. His hair seemed to stand on end. His ears burned. He couldn't stand the heat, the heat, the heat. A strange sensation shot from his head and raced down his spinal cord. Something whirled around his groin. And he sat up and moaned when something exploded out of his penis in an uncontrollable, embarrassing torrent, like preserved oil from a burst pipe.

The sheets were flooded by the deluge of wasted human seed. The woman tittered – 'Oh, holy man, holy man, what have you done?' – feeling the warm oil bathe her bare thighs. Ramu grabbed her impulsively, and let out a deep sigh.

'I'll have my cold drink and fruit now,' he croaked.

The Invisibles

It is a bright Saturday afternoon in Yeoville. We are at Ekhaya, our favourite watering hole, shimmering in our finery, chilling out there on the veranda, the better to spy on the passing parade of pretty faces, long sexy legs and mosquito waists. Yeoville on a Saturday afternoon is like Rodeo Drive in Los Angeles – if one is to believe what we impressionable South Africans are forced to watch on our television screens.

My eyes are trained on a short little thing, in an even shorter red mini-skirt, I'm making mental notes as always when I'm looking for material for a short story. Suddenly I spot Guz-Magesh tiptoeing up the steps that lead to the veranda where we're sitting. Pain is etched on his face. He is wearing sandals.

Before he can even find a chair, Guz-Magesh croaks in a tired voice, 'Giiiiift!' He is trying to get the attention of Gift, our alleged waiter who is always engrossed in a pile of Lotto tickets. 'Gift, you moerskont, get me a double Johnnie Walker Black and ice.'

Guz-Magesh is in so much pain, he doesn't even bother to greet us. He pushes Avocado Johnny out of a chair, and claims it as his own, plonking his considerable weight down.

Doctor Bones, resplendent in one of his shirts that many people have in the past mistaken for curtains, tries to break the ice: 'Guz-Magesh, you must cut back on red meat. Otherwise gout is going to kill you one of these days. Look at you, you can't even inhale and exhale without causing pain to your feet.'

'Fuck off, you fake doctor,' Guz-Magesh regains his voice. 'Who asked for your opinion? This is not gout. This is the doing of some people who hate me. They have bewitched me. I have been attacked by bouts of gout before, so I know what gout is. What I am suffering from today is not gout. This is bad medicine from an evil person. I tell you, they have bewitched me, just because I have been promoted at work. You can take a black man out of the bush, but you can't take the bush out of him, I tell you. The black man and all things dark and menacing are inseparable travelling mates.'

A century later, Gift delivers Guz-Magesh's drink, which the latter finishes in two hungry gulps. He orders another one. While we have Gift's attention, I suggest to the Dudman to order a plate of fried ox liver, which I know is the Dudman's preferred dish here at Ekhaya, this joint's menu being anaemic in the first place.

'There are many people who hate me around here,' Guz-Magesh says in an animated voice. The drink seems to have done him some good. 'Dudman, I think you are one of those people who hate me. How can you order red meat when you know very well that I can't eat it, considering the state I am in?'

'But I thought you just told us that it is not gout you are suffering from, that you have been bewitched?' the Dudman says, adjusting his spectacles.

'Don't play games with me,' says Guz-Magesh, wiping his sweating face with the back of his hand. 'I didn't say I wasn't suffering from gout. I said this gout that has taken charge of my feet is not normal gout; it is gout brought on by bad medi-cine, from a wizard or a witch. Yeah, I still say you can take a black man out of the bush, but you can't take the bush out of him. And I am not including Nelson Mandela in this sweep-ing statement. He was not a black man. He was a saint.' Having dispensed this piece of pedagogy, Guz-Magesh pauses to catch his breath. Then he continues, 'They have bewitched me so I can't enjoy good things like red meat, tomatoes and other goody-goody things for the palate.'

Gift brings our plate of ox liver. Like vultures, we descend on it. Guz-Magesh looks longingly at the meat, finishes his drink, and orders another one. When it becomes clear to him that we are single-minded in our determination to deal with this mound of meat, Guz-Magesh takes two pieces of liver. He chews. Then he winces, as if the meat has already descended to his feet, caus-ing him immediate pain. He takes two more pieces.

Guz-Magesh accepts his drink from Gift. He takes a sip, puts the glass down. And he says, 'You know, cats, for the larger part of my life, I had no truck with witchcraft. I didn't believe it existed. Until most recently, that is. And you know my first brush with witchcraft started when I came back from exile.'

Guz-Magesh is a former guerrilla fighter who spent years in Angola and Tanzania being trained for the Big War against the Apartheid Regime.

When the plate of liver is finished, Shemen orders a plate-ful of chicken feet. For my part, I always thought chicken feet were not supposed to be eaten by human beings. But when you arrive in Johannesburg from the coast, which is my ancestral home, you cast aside your coastal culinary prejudices, and go with the flow. I have to admit that, after experimenting with boiled chicken feet, I found them surprisingly refreshing to the palate.

The plate of chicken feet arrives. We attack it with gusto, teeth noisily crushing the tiny bones. Sucking sounds are heard all around as men lick gelatinous gravy from the chicken feet.

And what does Doctor Bones do? After watching us eat for a while, he reaches out for a fork and knife, which he uses to eat the chicken feet. I have never seen anything like this before. But Johannesburg is always full of surprises. It's no wonder he's so thin his shoulders look like coat-hangers. He is averse to food, as opposed to Shemen, who is always eating.

Anyway, Guz-Magesh continues with his tale:

When Guz-Magesh came back from exile, he was jobless. He was desperate for pocket money, cigarette money, booze money, and money that would make him respectable among the babes. A man with no mokotla doesn't appeal to the babes. A friend of his, Pule – who was equally penniless – came up with a great idea. He said, 'Guzzy, with all the skills you picked up in exile, you shouldn't be starving!'

'All they taught me in exile is how to shoot guns, how to plant bombs, and how to duck bullets,' Guz-Magesh told him.

'Exactly my point,' said his friend, Pule. 'You need to start shooting guns to make money.'

Guz-Magesh asked his friend what exactly he meant. And Pule explained that the thing to do when you are a penniless man with the know-how to shoot guns is to either rob banks, or hijack cars, which you then sell. Or hijack cash-in-transit vans. Pule said, in his opinion, hijacking cars could be messy because if you try to hijack a car driven by a stubborn person, you might end up having to kill that person. Robbing banks is tricky, what with all the security cameras. The only sensible thing is to hijack cash-in-transit vans.

Pule explained to an astounded Guz-Magesh how easy it is to hijack a cash-in-transit van. When you see the armed guards with their huge boxes of cash, you just walk straight to them, and grab the cash.

'But the buggers will shoot you even before you reach them!' Guz-Magesh said irritably.

'You are missing the point entirely!' said Pule. 'The guards can't see you as you approach them. Because you are invisible! That's how Sgonyela does it. You've seen Sgonyela's new BMW. And you know very well he is not gainfully employed. He buys these cars of his with money from his cash-in-transit gigs. Simple as that. But Sgonyela won't share his secret with anyone. He won't tell you how he gets to be invisible. But you know what, I have been doing a lot of research. That's what you do when you are starving. You become thoughtful. And one of the things that a thoughtful person does is to do some research that might alleviate his hunger. That's what I did: I did research. And my findings are illuminating.' Pule paused for effect. 'Guzzy, I have found a medicine man who has helped many cats become invisible. For a few hundreds of rand, he will render *us* invisible! It's just that I can't be invisible all by myself. I need a back-up. I will need your military training in case things go wrong. I need you to teach me a few basic things about guns, and I will take you to the medicine man who will make us invisible. Then we will triumph over those chaps who drive the money vans.'

Guz-Magesh was impressed by Pule's story, but in all honesty he thought Pule was under the spell of marijuana, of which he smoked a lot, and which tended to make him creative and talkative. Or hallucinatory? After all, where have you heard of medicine that can render a person invisible?

Four days later, Pule was at Guz-Magesh's door. He told his friend he had managed to scrounge some banknotes together. He was ready to take Guz-Magesh to the medicine man who was going to render them invisible. Guz-Magesh looked closely at his friend. No, the cat had not smoked yet, Guz-Magesh decided. This cat in front of him was dressed neatly, businesslike. Guz-Magesh thought very briefly about his friend's proposition. He realised that it was not his money that would go down the drain, so why not humour Pule and accompany him to the famed medicine man. Guz-Magesh thought: *Me and my cynicism from exile! Let's give this invisibility thing a try. Let's see where it takes us.*

They took a taxi to Thokoza men's hostel where the medicine man had his home. Gonondo, for that was the moniker of the medicine man, was dressed in khaki shorts, sandals made of discarded car tyres, and a leopard-print vest when they met him. They explained their business. Gonondo seemed familiar with their request. He said, 'My boys, don't make the mistake many young men like you make. Which is, don't forget about me once you've reached the kingdom of tycoons and billionaires. Don't discard me as soon as you've become rich thanks to my potent medicine. Give me a cut of your takings.'

He told them how to use the crushed herbs and foul-smelling animal fat that he handed over to them: 'Make sure you take the dosage I stipulate exactly,' Gonondo said. 'Swallow a pinch of the medicine I call sibindi uyabulala; pour a handful of sibindi uyaphilisa into your bath water; and smear this fat I call ngiyasabeka ungangiboni on your face.'

So, the two young men paid for the services, and hit the road. They knew not to say 'goodbye' to a medicine man when leaving his place. This would only undermine the potency of the medicine. All they did was wordlessly accept the medicine, pay the man, and get out of there – and they made sure to have a big scowl on their faces as they hastily vacated his premises. Everyone should see that you mean business when you leave a medicine man. And you can't mean business if you're smiling.

The following day, Guz-Magesh took his friend to the outskirts of their neighbourhood. This was a wooded area full of birdsong and animal noises. Not a human being in sight. A good place to do what they were about to do. Guz-Magesh opened the gunny sack he'd been carrying. There was an AK-47 and a Beretta, and some grenades inside. They spent the whole afternoon and some of the evening there. Guz-Magesh was teaching his friend how to use the various weapons. This military instruction went on for two weeks.

It so happened that during this time, Guz-Magesh got a piece job at a steel factory. He jumped at the opportunity. But the hijacking of cash-in-transit cars was still very much at the back of his mind. He had been doing research of his own, and had noticed that a number of childhood friends were into this racket. And they were eating very well, indeed. So he definitely wanted to hijack a car for himself at some point. But for the time being he took the poor-paying job, to create a cover for himself when he finally became rich and people wondered where he got the money from. He was thinking like a soldier

once again: always thinking ahead, always thinking of conse-
quences, cause and effect.

He was scrubbing the floors in the workshop at his place of
employment when the public address system called out his
name. The woman on the PA system said he had a visitor at
the gate. He was not expecting any visitors. In fact, he wasn't
allowed visitors unless it was an emergency. So he had to wonder who could have the gall to drop in unannounced. When
he got to the gate, who did he see but his good friend Pule!
Pule's face was unusually dark and very shiny. He whispered,
'Guzzy, am I still visible? Can you see me?'

Guz-Magesh said to him, 'What nonsense are you talking
about? Have you been smoking again?'

He whispered, 'No, my friend, I am dead serious. I used
the invisibility medicine before I got here. This is a trial run.
I have to check if it is working. Next week we hit our first
money truck, remember?'

'But, Pule, I can see you all right. Maybe you didn't follow
Gonondo's instructions down to the T...'

'But I did, my friend! I did. Remember, I've always been
good at memorising things. Remember you used to copy off me
when we were in school? Remember?'

Yes, Guz-Magesh did copy off Pule at school ... and they
were always at the bottom of the class.

'Tell you what,' Guz-Magesh said to him, 'go home and rest.
I will use the medicine on myself tomorrow and see how things
turn out.'

Indeed, the following day he used the medicine as instructed. He left his house and was disturbed that every person he
came across in the street greeted him heartily. *Why am I not*

invisible? he wondered. At work, his manager shouted at him: 'Fat boy, you must wash before you come to work. You stink to high heavens! And look at your face. What's this shiny stuff on your face?'

Guz-Magesh was thoroughly pissed off that he was still visible and, worse, attracting attention with the foul smell of the medicine man's concoction.

At the weekend, he went to Pule's house. After a short meeting, they agreed to go and confront Gonondo the medicine man about this vexing matter. When they got to the hostel, Gonondo was squatting behind the communal toilets, engaged in his daily self-induced vomiting ritual that is meant to cleanse one's system. Finished, the medicine man washed his hands under the tap, and led them to his room. Because he was a senior citizen at the hostel, and a respected medicine man to boot, he had his own room while ordinary hostel dwellers were squashed ten men to a room.

'Oh, great Gonondo, the medicine does not seem to be working,' Pule got to the point immediately.

'We are not undermining your powers, nor are we speaking ill of your reputation, but the medicine doesn't seem to be working,' Guz-Magesh tried to be diplomatic. He added: 'Maybe we did something wrong when we used the medicine.'

Gonondo cleared his throat, and spat a gob of phlegm on the floor. He said, 'You township boys are not good listeners. I told you to swallow a pinch of sibindi uyabulala, pour a handful of sibindi uyaphilisa into your bath water, and smear ngiyesabeka ungangibheki fat on your face. Always in that order. Make sure you take the dosage I have stipulated. When I say a handful, I mean exactly that.'

As Gonondo was talking, Guz-Magesh suddenly realised where the problem lay: the medicine man had huge fingers and massive hands. So, Gonondo's pinch could easily be a handful to the two young men. And the medicine man's handful could easily be a shovel-full. He raised this point with Gonondo. The medicine man said, 'Now, you have woken up from your slumber of stupidity. My hands are bigger than yours. So, use your head as you use my medicine.'

Gonondo continued to explain: 'Remember, you will only be invisible to your enemies – in other words, the people in the money van, or the staffers at a bank, if you want to take on a bank. The rest of your family and friends will be able to see you.'

The two young men went home, embarrassed that they had not followed the medicine man's instructions carefully. They decided to do a proper trial run. One Saturday, they took the medicine as instructed, smeared themselves with animal fat, and left for town. They chose a bank at random, and started making their way towards it. A security guard intercepted them at the door: 'Gentlemen, may I please search you?' He started patting them down. 'Phew!' he said. 'You guys must wash before you come to town. You give us black folks a bad name. White people always say we stink. And you are only confirming that. Be kind to our race, gentlemen. Mandela's legacy can't carry the race all alone. We have to play our part as well.'

The two young men exchanged angry glances, each silently accusing the other: *You didn't follow the instructions properly; that's why we are still visible!*

They walked to a teller's window. The woman at the window smiled brightly. 'Gentlemen, how may I help you?'

'We want to open a joint savings account,' said Pule.

'You need to bring your identity documents and, if you are employed, pay slips from your employer. Also, don't forget to bring a proof of residence – a utility bill would suffice.'

They thanked her, and walked out of the building. On the way home, a fight erupted: 'You have let me down once again,' Pule shouted. 'You didn't follow the instructions.'

'It's you who didn't follow the instructions,' Guz-Magesh retorted. 'I know you were sleeping with a woman last night. In terms of African medicine, you are not supposed to sleep with a woman the night before you use the medicine.'

'Gonondo never said anything about sleeping with women. You are making it up.'

'It's common practice among those who use African medicine not to sleep with women the night before they use the medicine. Sleeping with a woman renders the medicine impotent. Don't you know that?'

The young men parted on that angry note.

At Ekhaya, Guz-Magesh is telling us now: 'So, a week after our botched trial run at the bank, I was sitting at a watering hole in my hood. Somebody started screaming, "Hey, Guz-Magesh, that thin friend of yours is on TV. Pule is on TV! Come have a look. Quickly!" I rushed to the TV room. And there, on the screen, a body covered from head to toe with a white sheet was lying on the ground. The sheet was covered in splotches of blood. The person was clearly dead. In the top right-hand corner of the screen was a head-and-shoulders photo of Pule with a big smile on this face. The news reader was saying that Pule Monareng had been shot dead. She said that the lone robber had tried to snatch a huge box of money from a cash-in-transit van. The news reader told us: "Security guards and witnesses at the scene say the would-be robber was shouting: *I am invisible, give me the money! Don't even pretend you can see me. I am invisible!*"

Acknowledgements

'Talk of the town' was shortlisted for the 2018 Commonwealth Short Story Prize and first published in the Commonwealth Writers' online magazine, *Adda* (https://www.addastories.org/).

'Water No Get Enemy' originally appeared in Short Story Day Africa's 2015 anthology, *Water*, edited by Nick Mulgrew and Karina Szczurek.

'This Bus Is Not Full!' was first published in Short Story Day Africa's 2017 anthology, *Migrations*, edited by Efemia Chela, Bongani Kona and Helen Moffett.

'Beds Are Burning' was developed from an earlier short story, titled 'Legs of Thunder', which was shortlisted for the 2015 Commonwealth Short Story Prize.

An earlier version of 'Learning to Love', then titled 'Learning a New Language', appeared in the 2016 Short Sharp Stories anthology, *Die Laughing*, edited by Joanne Hichens and published by Tattoo Press.

'Ramu the Hermit' was first published in *The Finishing Touch: Stories from the 1991 Nadine Gordimer Short Story Award*, edited by Andries Walter Oliphant. It was later incorporated into Fred Khumalo's novel *Seven Steps to Heaven*, which was published in 2007 by Jacana Media.

About the author

FRED KHUMALO holds an MA in creative writing from Wits University and is also a Nieman Fellow (Harvard University, 2011-2012). He has been shortlisted for the Commonwealth Short Story Prize twice: for 'Legs of Thunder' in 2015 and for 'Talk of the Town' in 2018. Fred Khumalo's books include *Bitches' Brew*, *Seven Steps to Heaven*, *Touch My Blood* and *Dancing the Death Drill*. A stage adaptation of *Dancing the Death Drill* premiered at Nuffield Theatre in Southampton in 2018, and was performed at the Royal Opera House in London in 2019. He lives in Johannesburg.